Henry Edwards

A Mingled Yarn

Sketches on Various Subjects

Henry Edwards

A Mingled Yarn
Sketches on Various Subjects

ISBN/EAN: 9783743480858

Manufactured in Europe, USA, Canada, Australia, Japa

Cover: Foto ©Andreas Hilbeck / pixelio.de

Manufactured and distributed by brebook publishing software (www.brebook.com)

Henry Edwards

A Mingled Yarn

A MINGLED YARN

SKETCHES ON VARIOUS SUBJECTS

BY

HENRY EDWARDS
COMEDIAN

———

" The web of our life is of a mingled yarn, good and ill together."

.ALL 'S WELL THAT ENDS WELL.

———

NEW YORK

G. P. PUTNAM'S SONS
27 & 29 WEST 23D STREET

1883

Press of
G. P. Putnam's Sons
New York

DEDICATION.

PREFATORY NOTE.

I DESIRE to disarm all hostile criticism upon the contents of this book, by stating that it is solely in obedience to the wishes of friends that these simple sketches have been collected and placed before the public eye. No one knows better than I do their numerous blemishes, but I prefer to present them as they are, rather than to attempt their elaboration, conscious at least of the fact that their publication, if it do little good, can on the other hand be productive of no harm to any but the author.

HY. EDWARDS.

WALLACK'S THEATRE,
  NEW YORK, *Dec.*, 1882.

CONTENTS

THREE WEEKS IN MAZATLAN.

ON the 27th of December, 1874, accompanied by my wife, I took passage in the steamship "Montana," bound for Panama, and after rather a boisterous passage of four days, during which time we experienced as much misery as is usually accorded to sea-going people about the Californian coast, we ran into the harbor of San Diego, the future rival of San Francisco, as its inhabitants are pleased to call it ; a rising town, doubtless, but destined to remain for many years in its rising condition, before it can in any way compete with the mistress of the Golden Gate. The San Diegans point with pride to their safe and beautiful harbor, but they forget to mention that that harbor is always destitute of ships, one small coaling barque belonging to the P. S. N. Co., being the only vessel in sight upon our first visit, and on our return, even this one was absent, and the stars and stripes which floated from the custom-house, met no answering signal from the waters of the bay. The hopes of this place are at present wholly in the future, and they seem to depend upon the Great Southern Railway across the continent, of which it will be the western

1

terminus, and the completion of which must certainly one day make San Diego a place of considerable importance.   Steaming down the bay, and
past the substantial light-house erected on Point
Loma, we looked our last for a time upon green
grass and fertile fields, and for three days coasted
along the rough, rocky, and forbidding shores of
the Californian Peninsula, passing almost within
sight of the reef on which the ill-fated " Sacra-
mento " had so recently met her unfortunate dis-
aster; and crossing the entrance to Magdalena Bay,
the site of Drake de Kay's late colonization venture,
which settlement is now given over entirely to a
number of Ecuadorians, engaged in gathering or-
chilla, we rounded the curiously perforated rocks off
Cape St. Lucas and came to anchor there on the
eighth morning after our departure from San Francisco.   To all who have travelled to California by
the way of the Isthmus, this halting-place is familiar, and needs no remark here except a passing
notice of the recent death of the founder of the
settlement, Capt. Richie (" old Tom Richie," as he
was familiarly called), which took place about three
months before our arrival, and which, to those coast-
ing vessels accustomed to make the Cape a place of
call, could be regarded as no other than a national
calamity.   Richie was certainly a singular and uncommon man, full of the adventurous spirit which
distinguished the early pioneers of this coast, owning
a great and generous heart, which was always ready

to give of his abundance to those who needed it, and possessed of that peculiar faculty of mind which sees justice from an abstract point of view, and which does right from a consciousness of internal principle, rather than from the dictates of conventionality or the urgings of society's laws. When a lad of only seventeen years of age, he ran away from an English whaling ship, fixed on Cape St. Lucas as his home, lived there for upward of fifty years, married two Mexican wives (some people say seven), reared a large family of children, and, for the latter years of his life, was looked upon as an absolute king in his district—his word upon all matters in dispute being regarded as law, the opposing parties in his court being always satisfied with his verdict, and never appealing to a higher one for a new trial, as is too often the case in more advanced and polished communities. He seldom left his home, except now and then for a journey up the gulf as far as La Paz or Loretto, and on one occasion to San Francisco, the noise and bustle of which city proved too much for the old recluse, and he was glad once more to seek the seclusion of his peaceful home. Every sailor has a kind word for " old Tom Richie," and the tone of respectful sorrow which now accompanies the utterance of his name, is a sure indication that upon that barren spot at Cape St. Lucas, a kindly heart and active brain have found their last resting-place ; and that from above his tomb in the place he loved so well, will spring up in many a heart, gentle but abiding memories of the past, and grateful recollections of an old friend, long regarded, but now passed from earth away.

Leaving Cape St. Lucas, we steamed up the gulf until abreast of San José, a small settlement in a valley of plenty surrounded by desolation, hearing much of the pearl fisheries of La Paz and the oranges of Loretto (both which quaint cities lay to the north of us, but which, alas! were destined to be unseen by our eyes), and then headed our course straight across the gulf to Mazatlan. The pearl fishery at La Paz is a very productive source of wealth, last year alone yielding, as I am told, up-ward of $130,000 worth of pearls, some of which were of extreme beauty and quaintness of shape, one specimen obtained within the previous two months having been sold in Mazatlan for the large sum of $5,000. The diving is carried on wholly by Mexi-cans, who are adroit fishermen, and appear to relish their somewhat dangerous life. The shells from which the pearls are obtained are found in water from three to four fathoms deep, and it is somewhat singular that on the eastern side of the gulf no specimens of the pearl oyster have yet been dis-covered, the fishery being confined solely to the waters near La Paz. The pearls are said to be all profit to the company who are engaged in the speculation, as the shells themselves, which are ex-ported to Europe (where they are largely employed for inlaying and lacquer work), pay the total ex-

penses of the labor employed. The town of Loretto, to which I alluded, is highly celebrated for the
quality of its oranges, many of which find their way
across the gulf to Guaymas and Mazatlan, where they
command far higher prices than the fruit grown in
those places. Gradually losing sight of the land,
the good ship " Montana," pitching and rolling at a
fearful rate under the influence of a strong nor'-
wester, made rapid progress across the Californian
Gulf, and in twenty-two hours after leaving Cape
St. Lucas the booming of our gun awoke the echoes
among the hills and valleys which surround the
most important Pacific seaport of the Mexican Republic, and as we drop our anchor between the
rocky islands of Gervo and El Christon Grande,
our journey's end is reached, and we are safely at
rest upon the bright blue sea which washes the
walls of the strange city of Mazatlan.

It was a picture full of that strange and dreamy
beauty found only in tropical climes, which gives to
the spirit a sense of almost oppressive sadness ;
filling the heart with stifled longings for a better
understanding of its untold loveliness, and suggest-
ing to the soul a vision of that brighter and better
land "beyond the skies," which is the sustaining
hope of our earthly pilgrimage. Groups of low, flat-
roofed houses, curiously painted in white, blue, pink,
and yellow, surmounted by the giant stems of
cocoa-nut trees waving their finely cut branches in
the gentle breeze, and lighted up in front by the rich

transparency of the tropic sea, formed the foreground of the picture ; while beyond it stretched a series of broken hills, crowned to their very tops with dense and curious vegetation—a purple haze enshrouding their summits, and blending them into the obscurity of the distance. Through rifts in the mist which overhung the landscape like a veil, could be discerned the rocky forests crowning range after range of the great mountain chain which forms the backbone of America, and which reaches its grandest forms in the Rocky Mountains of the North and the Andes of the Southern Continent. Strange-looking trees of giant cactus covered the precipitous sides of the island and rocky points more immediately surrounding us, while flights of turkey-buzzards hovering like restless ghosts of the departed over the land, and groups of grand gray pelicans and graceful white cranes about the water, lent a living interest to the scene. Around and above all was shed the golden glory of a tropical sunrise, the most delicate purple tints shading off into richest crimson, and encircled by a greenish tinge of almost ethereal brightness, the slanting beams of the approaching luminary striking upon the dull green foliage, and illuminating it with transcendent splendor.

The city itself is built upon an isthmus, which at its narrowest point is not more than two hundred yards in width, the old town occupying the northern, and the new town (or that chiefly inhabited by the better class of residents) the southern portion. Southward, the peninsula rises into a high, rocky hill, on which are the remains of a once powerful fortress, which from its position offers a most important point of defence, but which, with that carelessness peculiar to the Mexican race, has been suffered slowly to crumble into decay. On the top of this eminence is the flag-staff station, and beyond it, still farther to the south, rises the rocky mountainous island called El Christon Grande, the highest peak of which I had subsequently the pleasure of ascending, and from which a grand and commanding view of the surrounding country is to be obtained. At the southwestern extremity of El Christon is a singular cave, the walls of which are strongly impregnated with sulphur, and lead off into passages in the heart of the mountain as yet unknown and unexplored. The peak of this interesting island seems formed by nature for a light-house station, and in the hands of any other people would certainly have been put to such a use, but it is a singular fact, and it may be here noted as one of great significance, and remarkably illustrative of the Mexican nation, that while they have during the past ten years collected upwards of two millions of dollars from various nationalities for light-house dues, and almost as much more for pilotage, there is not a single light-house on the whole Mexican coast, while the duties of a Mexican pilot appear to consist in going out in his boat to within three or four hundred yards of any vessel requiring his assistance, waving a white flag, and then quickly turning round and pulling back to the shore.

Having bargained with some good-looking boat-men to take us from our anchorage to the shore, a distance of about two miles, for the sum of two dol-lars, we effected our landing upon a very dilapidated wharf, and proceeded to the custom-house for the purpose of having our baggage inspected, but not having the appearance of dangerous or suspicious people, we were allowed to pass with very little trouble, and at once looked about for some dray or express wagon to convey our boxes to the hotel at which we were to take up our residence. But vehi-cles of any sort there were none; and I looked on with some interest, and not a little uneasiness, at seeing our various packages shouldered by a whole army of *cargadores*, one of whom lifted a heavy leather trunk, weighing not less than one hundred and fifty pounds, as easily as he would a packet of tea, and marched off, leading the way, apparently not in the least oppressed by his burden. These *cargadores* are among the institutions of the place, and the loads they carry would appear almost be-yond possibility. I subsequently saw a man carry-ing seven boxes of claret from a lighter up to the custom-house, a distance of over one hundred and fifty yards, and upon another occasion met one of them with a piano on his shoulders; but I had be-come so accustomed to them by that time, that I was by no means astonished at this feat. These wonderful burdens are supported on a pad which rests on the shoulders, the strap of which is passed round the forehead, which is thus made to bear part of the strain.

Some short time ago an attempt was made by an enterprising American to introduce express wagons and drays into Mazatlan, but their use was forbidden by the local government, on the plea that it would ruin the business of the *cargadores ;* and so our speculative friend had to reship his vehicles to New York, lamenting the want of the progressive spirit, which is so eminently characteristic of the Mexican people. The only carts now employed are rude, heavy, lumbering contrivances, each drawn by a single mule or donkey, poor, patient, enduring creatures, without whom the Mexican could not exist, and who have certainly solved the problem of how to do the largest amount of work on the smallest amount of food. Over rough roads, almost untenable by the foot of man, these powerful and intelligent beasts carry their heavy burdens, plodding carefully and always safely, over the most dangerous places, rewarded only by the croppings of the roadside, or occasionally by a handful of dried corn-stalks at the end of the day's journey. Yet I would not have it understood that the Mexican is cruel to his beast ; on the contrary, he drives him by words rather than by the whip, and a good understanding always seems to exist between the animal and his master.

I one day witnessed an incident illustrative of this 'fact. A little mule drawing a big cart laden with cases of wine, in turning the corner of a street, had come into too close quarters with a post placed there to protect the sidewalk, and had brought the vehicle to a sudden stand. The driver, instead of lashing the animal and cursing him, as is too often the case among other people, in the most unconcerned manner took out a cigarette, lighted it, leaned against the nearest door-post and began to smoke, in the intervals of the puffs, chaffing his donkey, and laughing good-humoredly at his attempts to free himself from his position. I should translate what he said as something like: "You are a pretty fellow —a nice mess you are in—don't ask me to help you —get out of it as you best can, I 'm in no hurry," etc., etc.—laughing all the time as the donkey pulled and pulled almost enough to break the post down. The poor little animal seemed to understand all that was said to him, and cocked his ears with a most knowing expression, then in a moment lowering them suddenly he seemed to comprehend the difficulty, and forcing his cart backward, he gave a sudden turn, and feeling himself free of the post, marched triumphantly on with his load, his master slowly following, lighting another cigarette, and applauding the performance. I applauded too, and walking over to the driver, extended my hand to him, saying: "Bravo, old fellow, that 's better than beating him." I forgot, however, that he did not under-

stand English, so I tried Spanish; however, he understood this still less, and I concluded to try no
more, so he offered me a cigarette, gave the usual
salute of " Adios, señor," and went lazily and mer-
rily up the street after his brave little mule.

The carts of which I have spoken have very high
wheels and short shafts, and the animals drawing
them all wear a saddle fastened to the shaft, in the
rudest manner, by a piece of cord, while the head of
the animal is perfectly free from every kind of trap-
pings, no bridle or traces being used. The driver
walks by the side of his mule, and directs his course
by words, very rarely using his whip, and then
only cracking it loudly, with a great show of tem-
per, within half a yard of the animal's ear. It is
no uncommon sight to meet a number of these animals coming into town, each laden with a pile of
corn-stalks, all cut closely off at the roots, and
sometimes as much as fourteen feet in height,
packed carefully on each side of the pack-saddle,
and tied together at the top, thus perfectly enveloping the little animals, and allowing only their head
and ears to be seen. As they travel along laden in
this way, they look, when viewed from behind, like
a moving army of gigantic corn sheaves, and present a singular and somewhat ludicrous appearance.
The mules and donkeys also do all the water-carry-
ing for the city, this invaluable element being
almost invariably obtained from the numerous fresh-
water lagoons on the outside of the city, and conse-

quently not being over-excellent in quality. A
large quantity of water is in some houses gathered
in the rainy season and stored in reservoirs for the
purpose, but the bulk of the population have to depend for their supply upon the water-carriers and
their mules, who parade the streets throughout the
day. Each mule carries four earthen jars, containing about three gallons each, the value of the contents of each jar being about equal to fifteen cents.
Much of this water is strongly impregnated with
decaying vegetable matter, and is scarcely fit for
use without being filtered.

The hotel in which we took up our quarters was
called the Hotel Nacional, and was, luckily for us,
kept by a person who understood English, and who
had passed some time in San Francisco. It was a
large straggling adobe building, with about twenty
rooms, built in the form of a square, the centre of
which was entirely open, and planted with curious
trees and shrubs. Into this square sometimes came
a drove of mules to feed, while their owners did the
same beneath the open piazza, surrounded by trellis-
work, which formed our dining-room. The sleeping
apartments of this establishment were about sixteen
to eighteen feet square and almost as many feet
high, with bricked floors and whitewashed walls, in
the corners of which huge spiders and cockroaches
made their homes by day, sallying forth at night
to prey upon whatever they could find. The
spiders, however, though formidable-looking ani-

mals, are quite harmless, and the cockroaches, though perfectly swarming in point of numbers, are only terrible to persons possessing weaker nerves than ourselves. In fact, I rather liked them, as I was enabled to pursue my favorite study of entomology without its usual accompaniment of a long walk, and I am happy to announce that I discovered at least one new species of cockroach, even in our sleeping chamber. It was to this room that we retired to rest after our first day's long and fatiguing walk about the city—rest, did I say? Ah! how little did it deserve that word! To the lover of a comfortable bed, in which the soft down gently closes round him, lulling him to repose, and compelling him, when the morning breaks, to turn again for a

" Little more sleep, a little more slumber,"

I would say, emphatically: "Go not to Mazatlan." There are no beds, the places which delude one to rest being simply iron cots, on which is stretched a piece of canvas, covered by a single sheet. This is what one lies *on*. Then comes another sheet, and a sort of coverlid more like an old window-curtain than any thing else. This is what *lies on us*, and this is all; no mattress, no feathers, no blanket, no any thing like comfort; the pillows as round and hard as if they had been turned out of a log of wood, into which it is quite impossible for even the hardest and thickest of heads to make the least impression. Then, in addition to this solemn mockery of a comfortable bed—that haven of rest which every tired mortal groans for, and enjoys so much—thousands of fleas take up their residence in each cot, and nip and bite like furies the whole live-long night, utterly eluding all your vigilance, and laughing to scorn your attempts to catch them. They are not, as in civilized countries, good, fat, healthy-looking fleas, such as take hold of you honestly, and give you a chance to catch them with the assistance of a moistened finger, but tiny, vicious, active little fiends, that give you a remarkably sharp bite, and then jump off to attack some other part of your body. It has been said that an ordinary flea will leap over two hundred times its own length. I am sure these proportions must be much increased in the case of the fleas of Mazatlan, as they are smaller and leap farther than any fleas I ever saw. During the intervals in which these tormentors were at rest, swarms of mosquitoes varied the amusement, and drew our attention in another direction. These mosquitoes attack without the slightest noise, settling down upon the face as lightly as a snow-flake, when bang goes their sharp proboscis deeply into your flesh, and down comes your hand with a terrible whack, only to miss the enemy and make you think that for the future you would prefer being bitten. Downright fatigue at last, however, overcame even the fleas and mosquitoes, and we slept, only to awake in the morning with aching limbs, not in the least refreshed by our repose. This first night in Mazatlan was by no means an exceptional one. We were doomed to experience many such, varied occasionally by a continual crowing of cocks, which commenced soon after sunset and continued until long after sunrise. Sometimes the dogs began a barking chorus, and kept it up at intervals throughout the night, and worse than all, occasionally a man with a hurdy-gurdy would be hired by some of the *cargadores* and others of the denizens of the wharf to grind out his miserable tunes the whole night through for their special gratification ; and sometimes a full band would come to serenade some fair *señorita* on her festal day, and rattle away till the dawn of morning.

On these occasions it is usual to invite the musicians into the house, and keep the merrymaking there, but if the revellers have made too free before their approach, as is often the case, this custom is dispensed with, and, in revenge, they proceed to greater libations, and bang and toot away until the blush of day sends them to their homes. These constant interruptions, added to the hard and miserable beds, render Mazatlan not a comfortable place in which to sleep, and justify the warning I have given to all who love their beds to stay away from that city. And yet, when we grumbled about our broken rest, we were always coolly told : " Oh, you will get used to it ; we all sleep like that in Mazatlan; it is too hot to sleep on beds or mattresses, and, as to the fleas, they are no worse than in other hot countries; they are always most troublesome to new-comers," and other such consolation as this. Now, as to the heat, we never felt it during the warmest day as uncomfortably hot, and at night could always have borne a pair of blankets. The thermometer stands, with little variation, in the winter season at about 75°, but in the rainy season, which sets in about the end of April and continues until October, it ranges from 110° to 125° in the shade.

During the winter months I can imagine no climate more beautiful and health-giving than that of Mazatlan. Balmy, clear, and fresh as the air always is, it is sometimes rendered even more agreeable by a gentle breeze from the sea, and, as the city is surrounded on three sides by the ocean, it matters not from which quarter the wind may blow, as a pure and fresh air is sure to find its way to all quarters. There are no violent winds, no fogs, no dust, and it is surely not Utopian to look forward to a not distant day when this place may become a sanitarium for the enfeebled and worn constitutions of our more northern clime, to which those broken down by over-work may retire for rest and change, and for a time imitate the dwellers in that genial climate in the pure enjoyment of their " *dolce far niente.*"

The streets of Mazatlan are crooked, narrow, and badly paved, but they, as well as the houses, both inside and outside, are kept scrupulously clean. A city ordinance obliges every householder once a year to paint, whitewash, or otherwise clean and adorn the outside of his house, and as this is usually done at the conclusion of the rainy season, we had the advantage of seeing the city in its new dress, the process of decoration having recently been completed. It is also compulsory upon every householder to keep the sidewalk and half the street opposite to his house perfectly and cleanly swept every morning, the carts for carrying away the dust and refuse calling each day for its removal. It is forbidden to throw dirty water about the streets under a penalty of five dollars; these enactments being in the chief streets of the city rigidly enforced, but in the suburbs, where sanitary regulations are not carried into effect, dirt accumulates in large quantities, and in some cases poisons the air to a considerable distance. The turkey-buzzards, so appreciated as scavengers in all tropical countries, here also perform their valuable offices, and being protected by the Government (their destruction being forbidden under a very heavy fine), they exist in enormous numbers, their gaunt and gloomy-looking forms, sad and melancholy as Poe's raven, being met with upon every side, both in the city and in its immediate neighborhood.

The houses are nearly all built after the same model, very few having more than the ground-floor, except in two of the principal streets and the plaza, where in some cases a second story has been added. The windows are generally without glass, and invariably barred with rods of iron, giving them a most prison-like aspect. The houses are always built to form two or more sides of a hollow square, the enclosed court-yard being given up to the cultivation of a garden, the Mexicans being extremely fond of flowers. Even when the absence of room or the means of the owner will not admit of a garden, a few flowers in earthen pots (roses, carnations, and balsams being the favorites) are the adjuncts to a Mexican home. It is not, however, unusual to find, even in the heart of the city—well-cultivated gardens, in which potatoes, lettuce, cabbage, radishes, and other vegetables of a colder clime, grow side by side with chilis, bananas, oranges, papayas, and other natives of the more tropical regions, the glorious cocoa trees always waving their graceful arms above the whole, like guardian spirits of the vegetable world.

The dwellings of the poorer class are mostly built of adobe and thatched with corrugated tiles, like those still remaining in many of the older settlements of California—of which some picturesque specimens still exist in Santa Clara and San José— while others are formed of boughs wattled together, and mud-plastered between, or of the branches of the cocoa-nut palm, interlaced on all sides so as to form a thatch, through which, however, in the rainy season the water pours without let or hindrance.

The cooking is always done on braziers or small ovens fed with charcoal, so that there are no chimneys, and consequently no smoke. Fires to warm the dwellings are quite unnecessary, even in the coldest seasons, and thus one of the terrors of our boasted civilization, which has of late years caused such fearful devastation throughout the land, has here no power, a conflagration being a thing unknown. Most of the houses, too, would fail to feed a fire; nothing but the rafters which support the roof, and the doors and shutters of the windows being built of any material which would burn.

The longest street in the city is the *Calle del Recreo*, which is about a mile in extent, and passes through one side of the principal plaza. The western end runs into the grand esplanade fronting on the ocean, called *Los Altos*, the favorite ride and promenade of the beauty and fashion of Mazatlan. Here are built some of the finest houses in the city, the dwellings of the wealthy merchants and others of the upper ten, furnished with exquisite taste, in which a generous and profuse hospitality is extended in the most refined and courteous manner. The city has three plazas, the principal one being oblong in form, about one hundred yards long, by fifty wide. The northern side is devoted to a hotel, and the rooms of the Mazatlan Club, an institution largely supported by the foreign residents, and which, if the favorite game of montè be not too rashly indulged in, will afford the visitor who is fortunate enough to gain access to its somewhat exclusive recesses, many pleasurable hours. One corner of the plaza is occupied by the offices of the telegraph company, a line having recently been carried across the continent, connecting the city of Mexico with the Pacific seaboard. Owing, however, to the frequent revolutions it is sometimes impossible to get a message through, as each party, as it comes into power, thinks it its bounden duty to destroy the wires and poles. An instance is on record, however, in the times of peace, of a message occupying six weeks to reach Durango, a city about one hundred and thirty leagues from Mazatlan, so that, with such management, the telegraph service of Mexico would appear to be of little public benefit.

The plaza is, or rather was, surrounded by orange trees, for many of them have been allowed to go to decay, and no thought of replanting them appears to have existed. Those that remain are vigorous, healthy trees ; at the time of our visit two or three being laden with fruit in every degree of ripeness, while some were just bursting into flower. Some curiously carved stone benches, looking like the remains of the Aztecs, are built around the square, but the seats have been broken from many of them, leaving only the backs standing, and, with the true spirit of Mexican carelessness they will be suffered gradually to crumble away, when a little mortar and a few hours' work would restore them to their origi-

nal condition. Near the plaza, is an imposing-look-
ing building, one of the first which strikes the eye
of the visitor as he approaches the city from the
bay, which was intended for an opera-house, but,
owing to the death of its projector, on his voyage
from San Francisco, it has never been completed,
and is now entirely given over to the pigeons and
turkey-buzzards, who make of it a roosting-place.
The internal arrangements are made with considerable taste, the auditorium consisting of a large par-
quette, capable of seating about four hundred persons, the upper portion of the house being divided
into four tiers of boxes, each enclosed with elegant
designs in iron-work, now in many cases displaced
from their position and thrown to the ground to
rust and decay. The roof has been pierced for the
reception of a chandelier, and there is everywhere
evidence of the best intentions as to the adornment
of the building. The workmen had so far advanced
with their labor (when the sudden death of the proprietor brought the work to a conclusion), that a few
hundred dollars would suffice to finish it, yet no one
has been found with enough public spirit to take
the matter in hand, and this, one of the most im-
posing structures in the city, has therefore written
upon it the sentence of decay.

The people of Mazatlan are not, however, entirely without amusements. There is a small
theatre, or rather a hall with a stage at the end of
it, where dramatic and other performances are occa-

sionally given, which are always well patronized and
enjoyed by the audience. The Mazatlan stage boasts
of a few excellent local artists, the style of acting
most in vogue being that of the modern conversa-
tional school. The theatre is decorated with excellent portraits of some of the more eminent drama-
tists of Europe, among whom I noticed Shakespeare,
Molière, Lopez de Vega, Cervantes, and Byron.
There are many customs connected with the drama
in Mazatlan which are rather disagreeable to a
foreigner. In the first place, every man smokes
during the whole entertainment, enveloping the
whole place in a cloud of that vapor which was
so offensive in the nostrils of His Majesty James
the 1st of blessed memory. Then, the performance, which is advertised to commence precisely
at eight o'clock, rarely begins before nine, while
the waits between the acts are simply intolerable ;
a play of three acts, which could easily be finish-
ed by ten o'clock, in all cases lasting up to half-
past eleven, and sometimes much later. But Mexicans
are never in a hurry, and "*poco tiempo*" and "*mañ-
ana*" are the words in their vocabulary most frequently in use. I should also mention that, except
on particular occasions, programmes of the performance are rarely issued, publicity being given to the
same by a band parading the streets during the day.

The ladies attend the theatre in modern American costume, discarding their own graceful and becoming *rebosa* for a vile imitation of the worst

fashions of their neighbors, spoiling the appearance of their own usually waving, long black hair by those horrible excrescences called chignons, and utterly destroying the character of their clear olive complexions by plastering them with paint and pearl powder.   The poorer class are great lovers of the theatre, and will live upon nothing, and go with bare feet for weeks, in order to save the treasured *dos reales* which shall give them the entrance to their favorite amusement.   They seem to relish keenly every joke uttered by the actors, and applaud every point with infinite zest and good humor.

We found the evenings sometimes rather lonely in Mazatlan, and upon one occasion, when the theatre was closed, we visited a grand panorama professing to give us correct representations of the principal cities of Europe and America.   From the flourish of trumpets which accompanied the announcement, we expected something at least tolerably good ; we saw a miserable peep-show, lighted by two sputtering oil lamps, and consisting of a series of magnifying bull's-eyes, through which we viewed the wonderful pictures gathered at great cost by the proprietor.   A wretched hand-organ behind the scenes, which every now and then stopped suddenly, in spite of the vigorous manipulation of its owner, and then as suddenly went on again, taking up the tune some sixteen bars beyond where it left off, was the sole accompaniment of this wretched swindle. But worst of all was the view of San Francisco. Now, I have never been to Lisbon or Palermo, and therefore I might be imposed upon as to the external appearance of these cities, but I do know something about San Francisco, and when I saw some impossible city, in which a huge elephant paraded the suburbs, while a gigantic ostrich stalked calmly by his side, I began to think that the proprietor's views of natural history were somewhat mixed, and to wonder what ideas the rising generation of Mexico would form of the natural productions of the Golden State. We left the grand panorama in disgust, and did not visit it again during its stay in the city.

The principal stores are elegant in their appointments and contain an excellent assortment of goods of all kinds ; the prices, as far as we could judge, being much the same as those of San Francisco, except for linens and silks, which were very much lower. There are no shop-windows in which to display the goods, and no posters whatever about the walls to intimate where certain articles are to be purchased, so that the intending customer has to seek somewhat industriously for whatever he may require. There are no newspapers in which to advertise, those published being simply small broadsheets of daily news, generally in part, if not wholly, controlled by the government, and the shopkeeper has therefore to depend upon his reputation and the absolute wants of the community for the sale of his wares. There are few manufactories on the Pacific coast of Mexico; sombreros, serapes, pottery, and harness-work being the principal productions. We saw several very elegantly mounted saddles and bridles, some profusely ornamented with silver, a Mexican taking great pride in the adornments of his charger. Within the last few years an American gentleman named Howell has established a cotton factory in Mazatlan, which appeared to do a very paying business. The cotton is grown in the interior and brought in its raw state to Mazatlan, where it undergoes all the processes of cleaning, ginning, spinning, and weaving into manta, or unbleached calico, of which the jackets and trousers worn by the Mexicans are invariably made. The labor is all performed by Mexicans, who in time make excellent operatives, a number of boys of ages ranging from eleven to fifteen being among the brightest of the whole. The wages paid are miserably small, thirty-seven and a half cents a day being the average amount, out of which the poor people have to find themselves. One dollar a day is the pay of the foreman of the establishment, who, at the time of our visit, was an American, very anxious to return to his native country. Large quantities of the calico find their way to Durango and Chihuahua, where it is sold at the rate of about eight dollars for a bale of forty yards. Close to this establishment is a match factory, also owned by an American, where matches of an excellent quality are made in large quantities, and find a very ready sale. Mr. Howell and his brother had recently obtained a charter to light Mazatlan with gas, an improvement for which the inhabitants ought to have been eternally grateful, but I regret to say that the speculation proved any thing but remunerative, and that the Messrs. Howell were yearly heavy losers by the transaction. Before the introduction of gas, the streets of the city were continually the scenes of outrages and robberies, sometimes accompanied by brutal violence; now such occurrences are, to say the least, uncommon, and on the whole good order and decency prevail. A policeman with loaded musket and a lighted lantern stands at the corner of every street, and after nine o'clock in the evening whistles loudly every half hour, thus serving a double purpose, by intimating the time of night, and giving evidence of his presence. He is never allowed to leave his post, so that in Mazatlan, at least, a policeman is always to be found when wanted. In addition to this force, mounted police, well armed, parade the streets during the day and night, by their presence awing the desperadoes, and enforcing the strictest quiet and order throughout the city.

I have spoken of the existence of two other plazas, one of which is situated in the old town, and is now rapidly falling to ruin. The hospital, which is a most melancholy place, suggestive of every horror which can afflict the human frame, occupies one end of it, and might readily be taken for a prison, its

dark and gloomy portals admitting not a ray of sunshine, while through the iron bars of their dismal
dwelling, the poor inmates, in every stage of disease, stare longingly at the street without, and
beg an alms from the passers by. This was
the saddest sight we saw in Mazatlan, and its
recollection must remain fixed upon our minds.
The other plaza is called the Plaza el Toros, and has,
as its name implies, occasionally been devoted to
bull-fights; the sport of which the Spanish races,
wherever found, are inordinately fond, but it is now
in a state of dirt and neglect. A little beyond
this plaza lies the cathedral of Mazatlan; not such
an edifice as is often found in Spanish America, in
which architectural grandeur is heightened by the
most lavish and costly decoration, but a miserable,
whitewashed, tumble-down place, containing a few
tawdily dressed figures; a worn-out table-cloth, decorated with shells and spangles, serving for the
covering of the altar. The floor is of brick, worn
into holes by the feet of the many devotees, and
the wood-work of the interior is everywhere perforated by insects, and fast crumbling into dust.
An attendant in a white jacket, looking like the
waiter of a hotel, who begged from us as we came
away, was the sole occupant of the place at the time
of our visit, and, indeed, we learned upon inquiry,
that the claims of religion are little recognized, at
least by the rich portion of the inhabitants of
Mazatlan. The women always on Sunday morn-

ings dress themselves in their very best and most showy costume, and go regularly to matins, but beyond this, little attention to religious duties seems to prevade the community. A few years since, the host was carried publicly through the streets, the priest following, decked in his gayest robes, while the festal days of all the saints in the calendar were faithfully and strictly observed. The accession of Juarez to power, however, destroyed the influence of the priests, and drove them from the cities to seek "fresh fields and pastures new." Now two alone remain in Mazatlan, and these are unobtrusive gentlemen, who accept matters as they are, and quietly make the best of them. At a little distance from the church, stands what there is of a grand cathedral, commenced some seven years ago, upon which upwards of $17,000 have been expended, but which remains, and is likely to remain, in an unfinished state, given over, like the theatre, to the rats, bats, and turkey-buzzards which everywhere swarm throughout the streets of the town.

It is noticeable that the two largest and most important buildings in the whole city, the cathedral and the theatre, should remain unfinished, and be suffered gradually to moulder away, as appears to be their inevitable destiny. Beyond these there are few public buildings of any importance, the barracks of the soldiers being nothing more than a collection of large adobe huts built in the form of a square, while the prison is a miserable den open to the street, the inmates secured by iron bars, behind which, unless confined for some very serious offence, they laugh and joke and drink with those of their comrades who enjoy their freedom. The tenants of the prison at the time of our visit were mostly soldiers, who were incarcerated for drunkenness and other petty offences, and who seemed to treat their imprisonment with all the levity at their command. These soldiers are a most repulsive-looking lot of fellows, idle, drunken, and dissolute; they wander about the streets in large bodies, sometimes of thirty or forty strong, clad in uniforms of what once might have been white calico, but which is now so begrimed with dirt, and generally in such a state of rags, that Falstaff's regiment would seem a well-dressed crowd beside them. They are the terror of quiet and respectable people, and as they pass along it is usual to give them as wide a berth as possible. If it so pleases them, they enter a store and call for *mescal*, which for peace and quietness the proprietor is bound to give them, and after a day's debauch, the materials for which have been thus easily obtained, they not unfrequently proceed in a body to the grand esplanade, of which I have spoken, and perform their ablutions in the bay, close to the dwellings and immediately under the eyes of most of the more refined inhabitants of the city. It is useless to protest against their outrages, as no redress could be obtained, and to resent any insult offered by them, would at any time be fraught with considerable danger, as a Mexican never forgives, and either by himself, or by the hands of his friend, would watch an opportunity to have his revenge when none were near to tell the tale. I had been told a number of rather alarming stories of the doings of these fellows during the first days of our stay, and as I never had very strong military proclivities I was always glad to get out of their way. If we saw them coming one road, we invariably went another, and for a long time contrived to avoid them, until on a Sunday morning, on which day nearly the whole force in the barracks are allowed their liberty, we came full tilt upon about a hundred of them, some of them half drunk, and all more or less under the influence of liquor, singing and shouting and rolling along the street, the very impersonations of dissipation in its worst and most brutal form. They were accompanied by some women, almost as degraded-looking as themselves, who had also apparently been paying attention to the "rosy," and I confess I almost trembled as I saw no hope of turning out of their way. There was nothing for it but to pass right through the crowd, so putting a bold face on the matter, we walked boldly toward them, and hardly knew where we were until we found ourselves in their midst. I began to wish myself safe at the hotel, from which we were considerably more than a mile distant, and experienced something of that feeling which lives among my memories as a boy, in which a cold shudder running down the back, and a gradual elevation, one by one, of all the hairs of the head, used to follow the relation of some horrible ghost story.

Suddenly the whole army stopped, as if about to make a concerted attack upon us, whispering to each other and pointing toward us in a most suspicious manner. I quickened my pace, but at the same time turned boldly to face the enemy, when I saw upon the countenances of all nearest to us, an expression in which curiosity and wonderment were strangely mingled, and instead of frowns and threatening looks, a half-grim smile pervaded the features of all. They were whispering to each other and pointing at my wife, and I caught among other words, those of one fellow, evidently the wit of the party, shouting at the top of his voice: "*La señorita!*" They then burst into a loud horse-laugh, amid the enjoyment of which we passed on our way. The cause of their surprise and laughter was the large sun-hat which my wife wore, and which, as I learned afterward, procured her the title throughout Mazatlan of "the lady with the umbrella on her head."

With the exception of my friends, the military, the population of Mazatlan is by no means given to drunkenness, and among fourteen thousand people the best possible order usually prevails. The liquor most in use among them is the different grades of spirit extracted from the Agave, or American aloe (*Agave Mexicana*), and known under the names of *pulque, mescal* (a contraction of *Mexical*), *maguay,* and *tequila.*

The best quality, which is very rarely to be obtained (as the Mexicans, among the few arts which they have borrowed from their more civilized neighbors, have learned to perfection that of adulterating liquors), is a pleasantly-flavored spirit, with a mixed taste of Peruvian Italia, and Scotch whiskey, and is probably very intoxicating if drank in sufficient quantity. A large revenue is derived by the government from the tax on this production, the chief quantity of which is made in the interior of the country. The several species of aloe are of remarkable value to the Mexicans, and are turned to a variety of uses, the fibre making a very strong and durable cordage, the refuse of the leaves being formed into paper of a coarser quality, and the juice of the young stems into excellent soap. In addition to this, the most impenetrable fences are made of the agave and cactus combined, which have the double advantage of growing more and more impenetrable as they increase in age. Over all the rocky hills and islands near Mazatlan some species of agave grow in considerable abundance, their dark-green foliage, terminated by sharp spines and surmounted by their grand spike of yellowish, sweet-scented flowers, being among the first objects to excite the attention of the stranger. In the market-place of the city may be found a number of the products of this mescal plant, and nearly every Mexican who can afford it, keeps his own still for the distillation of his favorite beverage.

The market is one of the interesting features of the place, and among the first spots to which the visitor directs his attention. It fills up a large square or block close to the unfinished cathedral of which I have spoken, the stalls being arranged in rows, the meat sellers occupying the chief part of the centre. Here may be found, at all seasons of the year, excellent lettuce, onions, radishes, turnips, and other familiar vegetables, while dried beans, or frijoles, singular-looking fruits, gourds of all shapes and sizes, and the ever-present chilis, attract the native population. The meat is cut into long strips, in a manner quite unknown to us, and looks as if it were intended to be sold by the yard; pork, of a very superior quality, and beef, being the most common. A good leg of mutton, or a porter-house steak, is a thing unknown in Mexico, and the manner of cooking utterly destroys our ideas as to how our meats should be eaten. The breed of sheep most in favor appears to be a long-horned, coarse-wool breed, which do not readily take on fat, and are therefore not the best kind for the butcher. Occasionally a deer makes its appearance in the market, and finds a ready sale; and more rarely, the carcass of the curious little animal, the armadillo, whose body is covered by a horny shield, is brought in from the country districts, and is in high favor with the Mexican gourmand. A living specimen of this very singular and interesting creature was one day brought to our hotel, and tied by its leg to a post in the court-yard. In a day or two it became quite familiar, and was a perfect pet among the people stopping in the place, enjoying the society of man, and always putting up its nose to be rubbed when any one approached it.

One morning, just as we were preparing for our first meal, we heard a cry of pain, which sounded almost like a human voice, and on inquiring the cause, learned that poor little armadillo had just suffered the death penalty, and that his body was to be served up to us that day for dinner. Under other circumstances I should have been glad to know something of the taste of the flesh, but to feed upon the body of a creature which, only a day before, we had caressed and petted, was more than we could stand, and with the death-cry of the little wretch ringing in our ears we passed him by untasted. Fish of various species and of excellent quality are always to be found, and plenty of chickens find their way into the market, but when placed upon the table they are usually so tough (for they never kill any thing but the old fowls) that I can say but little in their favor. Very few potatoes are as yet grown in Sinaloa, those used being nearly all imported from San Francisco, and retailing at the high price of twelve and a half cents a pound. Butter is remarkably scarce and very high in price, none whatever being produced in the state, but brought also from San Francisco, and doled out very sparingly to whomsoever may require it. Nevertheless, we constantly met on the outside of the city large droves of well-shaped, finely bred cattle, capable of producing any quantity of milk and butter, but seldom or ever put to this useful purpose. These cattle are naturally quiet and manageable, but have been rendered quite the reverse by the bad treatment of their owners. If a Mexican wants to do any thing, milk a cow, for instance, he generally contrives to go the farthest way round to accomplish his purpose. In the case of this commonplace operation, the services of not less than six men are required : one to lasso the animal, another to each of her horns, one to each hind leg, and one to milk ; the gentleman with the lasso, after having secured the beast, usually lighting a cigarette and holding the calf. It is no wonder that the poor animals object to the process of milking, and that they become restive and unmanageable under this system of treatment. The milk is of fair quality, and is sold about the streets at twenty-five cents a quart, the cry of "*leche*" being one of the first to greet the stranger's ear.

The morning after our arrival, we were of course very anxious to be away on our travels as early as possible, and rose with the sun, determined to lose no time. We sat at our table in the piazza and called for our breakfast. A cup of coffee and a small loaf of bread, with a sort of microscopic shaving of butter on the rim of a saucer, were brought us, and we just tasted these while the substantials were getting ready. After spending nearly half an hour over this introduction to our meal, I began to think that this was rather too much waste of time, and called out to our English-speaking friend, to know when breakfast was coming. "Oh," said he, "that's all at present, we don't have breakfast till half-past ten; this is the custom of the country, and you only get the cup of coffee or chocolate to stay your appetite till the morning's meal." My countenance fell. I knew that in Mexico, punctuality is not a prominent virtue, and that half-past ten might mean eleven, and the glorious butterflies, which I hoped to catch long before that time of day, faded from my mental vision. But we made up our minds to submit quietly to every thing without a murmur, and walked out to explore the city until the hour for refreshment arrived. The meal was a good one when it came, and we soon became used to these at first inconvenient hours. Our daily routine was to rise at daybreak, stroll about the streets or the market, make little purchases, or visit any places of note until breakfast, after which we usually took a carriage and drove for a few miles out of the city, spent the day in catching butterflies, gathering plants or collecting shells, and walked quietly home by about five o'clock, the hour for the hotel dinner. When I say a carriage, I allude to one of the lumbering hacks of the place, a sort of seedy barouche, with a covering of oil-cloth to protect us from the sun, drawn by a couple of horses, sometimes mules, and driven by a civil and obliging Mexican, who soon became accustomed to our ways, drove us into good places for our sport, and usually charged us half a dollar for a drive of about a couple of miles.

Upon two other occasions we went for a drive with some friends, when we penetrated for a considerable distance into the country, and returned with heightened impressions of its beauty. On one of these, we rode in a sort of spring wagon, covered with canvas, with seats for six persons, and drawn by five white horses, three in front and two at the pole, our equipage causing no inconsiderable stir in the streets of Mazatlan. The harness, it is true, was not highly ornamented, and was tied in some weak spots with pieces of tape and packthread, but the horses were full of spirit and rattled us along the excellent road for some twenty miles in a glorious style. It takes two men in Mexico, however, to drive a team, one to hold the reins and crack the whip, and the other to help by shouting and pelting the horses with small cobble-stones, a number of which he carried in a rawhide bag beside him on the seat. If the horses lagged a little, or came to a bad place in the road, this gentleman would jump off the box, run alongside them for a few yards, start them into a gallop, then remount his seat with the greatest ease, and continue the enjoyment of his cigar. In this way he performed some really difficult feats, and would certainly have made his fortune in a circus. Upon another occasion, an American gentleman who owns a buggy and pair, one of the few in the city, was kind enough to invite us to join him in a ride, and we looked forward to a spin behind a fast pair of trotters. We were doomed to disappointment; the buggy was a double-seated one, well built and roomy, but the horses were the most miserable pair of bare-boned, broken-down wretches I ever saw, out of whom to get more than four or five miles an hour would be an impossibility. Of course we said nothing, but after we had ridden a mile or two, and our friend had used up his arm in flogging and urging the poor animals along, he said to me, " I suppose you wonder why I drive such a miserable pair as this? " I modestly replied that I did not think they came of thorough-bred stock. "No," said he, " I should think not; they are the worst brutes I could find in the district. I used to pride myself upon good horses, and had, until the last revolution, a very fast team, but some of the rebel generals, when they took possession of the city, took also a fancy to them, and one day sent down and confiscated them. I bore this with as good grace as I could, and bought another pair, still better and faster, but upon the rebels being recently driven out, and the party of

the government coming into power, one of the
officers set his eye upon my team, said they were
wanted for military purposes, and sent some soldiers to take them from my stable up to his own
quarters. To be bitten twice in this way was
enough, so I thought that little game ' played out,'
and now I drive a pair that it is not worth any-
body's while to steal." This little incident, which
I relate in almost the words of my friend, will serve
to show you how much security there is for property
in the city of Mazatlan. It is well for me to mention here that the roads leading from Mazatlan were
at this season of the year in capital order, and except in some places near the sea, which were occasionally flooded at high tides, would bear very
favorable comparison with many of the roads in
California, the track running for miles through
what was once an almost impenetrable forest without encountering a stump or a hole. They are
never metalled, and their excellent condition is probably in part owing to the porous nature of the upper
soil, which never, even in the rainy season, when the
water pours down in floods, suffers it to remain long
upon the surface.

We found some excellent collecting in the vicinity of the town ; but when our walks were confined
to the immediate neighborhood, we were always
followed by a troop of children, who thought our
butterfly-hunting glorious sport, and entered into it
with more energy than I ever saw them display on

other occasions. They ran here and there, rushing after the unfortunate insects with their hats, crushing them out of all recognizable shape, and bringing them to me with an air of the most profound triumph. They would call out to their friends at the neighboring huts, and soon half a dozen of them would be increased to twenty.

One day I found a most curious and beautiful wasp's nest, covered with its living inhabitants, and was endeavoring to·secure my prize, taking full precautions against being stung, when the young urchins destroyed my sport by pelting the nest and the wasps with stones, spite of all my protestations, depriving me of every specimen and breaking the nest into a thousand pieces. This was too much for me to bear, and I accordingly told them to "vamoose," which, with much reluctance, they at last did. After this, they used to follow us at a distance, and catch insects on their own account, and it is more than probable that by this time many hundreds of butterflies have fallen to their sombreros. These children were bright-eyed, open-faced little fellows, revelling in dirt and freedom, but without any of that furtive and designing look which is too often the accompaniment of their older relatives. They, as all of the male sex, wear jacket and trousers of thin white calieo, with wide sombreros, more or less ornamented, mostly made of straw. The men wear the serape, or blanket, many of which are of brilliant colors, and extremely picturesque and ornamental.

The women, when young, are remarkably pretty ;
their dark and speaking eyes, long eyelashes, and
usually white teeth, lighting up faces of strong
expression; while their black hair, always well
combed and glossy, with their graceful and well-
shaped forms, moulded in all the luxuriance of a
tropical climate, combine to make them abundantly
attractive to a stranger's eye. They appear, however, to fade very early, and at about thirty years of
age they lose all traces of their former beauty, while
among the elder members of the sex may be found
some veritable hags, such as with little alteration
would serve for the witches of " Macbeth," or the
Fates of Michael Angelo. The dresses of the
younger women are usually of very pretty patterns, the products of French looms, and hang
gracefully over their well-moulded forms ; their
walk, like that of all people free from the trammels
and restraints of fashion, being free, erect, and firm.
A white chemise, not always concealing the upper
part of the body, and a black or gray *rebosa* complete their costume ; the ever-present cigarette, and
the tobacco stains upon their lips and fingers, giving
evidence of their love for the soothing weed. They
are invariably affable, courteous, and kind, and we
never paused to look through the door-way of a house,
without being invited to enter, to take the best seat
the dwelling afforded, and to inspect every thing of
interest which it contained. They are remarkably
fond of pets, and no hut, however poor, is without

its parrot, dog, or cat, while the pigs are generally allowed to share the hospitalities of the mansion. They appear to do a considerable share of the usual labor which is the lot of the poor, though in no case did we see women carrying heavy burdens, beyond their purchases from the market, and, on the whole, they looked as if they were well treated and contented with their lot. The making of the everlasting tortillas, the chief article of food of the lower classes, appeared to be their chief occupation. These tortillas are the pulpy paste of hulled corn, ground by hand, by a block of hewn lava about a foot long and three inches in thickness, upon a stone trough placed at an angle of about 45°. After the paste has attained its proper consistency, it is beaten out by the hand into round flat cakes, and then baked upon a hot stone. Occasionally, among the better class, a most delicate and palatable dish is made of these tortillas by adding chopped meat, grated cheese, finely cut onions, peppers, and tomatoes, with a dash of garlic added ; and the proper mixture of the ingredients for the *enselados*, as they are called, is the chief triumph of the culinary art. The pottery used in every Mexican household is of remarkably pretty designs, reminding one of some specimens which are brought from Pompeii. It is of hard finish, and very clear and strong. It is mostly made far in the interior, and when we consider that it has to be brought for hundreds of miles over the mountain roads, it is astonishing that it can be sold at so reasonable a rate; as a whole assortment of sizes, shapes, and patterns, numbering about fifteen or sixteen pieces, can be purchased for a dollar. In these are cooked the chilis and frijoles, a kind of dark-red bean, which, with the tortillas, form the leading article of diet with the humbler classes. The plants on which these beans grow, are most beautiful climbers, with large bunches of lilac and crimson flowers, and pods, when fully developed, twelve inches in length,—plants which grow almost wild in every garden, but which would be an ornament to any conservatory. Upon our collecting trips we often visited some of the small gardens attached to the dwellings of the poorer people, and never without being invited to carry away specimens of any thing which the place afforded.

There were only about twelve Chinese in Mazatlan, at the time of our visit, and these all filled the positions of cooks, so that the washing was done by women, who make use of the water of one of the large lagoons about a mile from the city for the purpose. A hundred of them may be seen sitting on the banks, themselves but little encumbered with clothing, chatting pleasantly over their work, while some soldiers, totally divested of their apparel, may be taking a bath and at the same time washing their horses close by. We had wandered, soon after our arrival, near to this lagoon, and had caused a considerable amount of destruction among the insect tribes, when we suddenly encountered a rather sar-

donic-looking Mexican, who appeared interested in
our pursuits.   He followed us for a considerable
distance, always keeping pretty close to us, and when
I stopped to pin a butterfly, poking his sombrero
close under my nose to watch my movements, per-
sistently telling that "*muchos grandos mariposas*"
were to be found a little further on.   "Further on"
we went, the *grandos mariposas* luring us away, until
we found ourselves close to the cemetery, far
from every habitation, and with no human being
besides ourselves in sight, or within half a mile of
us.   Our companion would not be cast off, but stuck
so closely to us, that my wife began to feel alarmed,
and suggested our return home, saying that there was
no one near us but his own countrymen, and that they
would be sure to help him, and adding, by way of a
clincher: "You know, Harry, your Spanish is so
awfully bad that they can't understand you, and
they might rob or murder us without its being
known."   I said: "Oh, nonsense—it 's all right;
where 's the money?"   "Oh, that 's safe enough,"
said she, when suddenly it occurred to me that we
were, perhaps, giving him a hint as to what was best
for him to do to us, and I said in a whisper:
"Suppose the beggar speaks English."   This was
enough.   Our butterfly-hunting was spoiled for that
day, so we turned and retraced our steps toward the
city.

Perhaps, after all, we wronged that Mexican
by our suspicions, and he may have followed us

from a real interest in our pursuit, and to gather a little knowledge on a subject hitherto a sealed book to him. We soon arrived on the high-road and among a number of people, and felt more at our ease; but our friend did not leave us until we came face to face with a custom-house officer carrying a drawn sword (notched and very rusty), who spoke English, and with whom we had previously formed a slight acquaintance. Upon meeting him, our companion of the morning slunk off toward the sea-beach, and was soon lost to sight among some bushes. Our custom-house friend told us that he was guarding the highroad with a view to preventing the entrance of any contraband goods, but I suppose finding our society more agreeable than his own solitary walk, he left the road to take care of itself, and accompanied us back to the city. As he spent three mortal hours in our society, I do not feel at all clear as to how the smuggled goods, if any, were prevented from entering the city during his absence.

The Mexicans are great people for levying duties, and immediately outside of the city are stations at which officers are always placed to collect taxes upon all kinds of produce going in or out of the city. They levy both ways, the poor charcoal-carrier having to pay for his mule's burden as he goes into town, and for the corn which he takes back for his family food as he goes out of it. The merchants, too, frequently suffer in the matter of duties.

During one of the recent revolutions, the rebels drove the government forces out of the city, and then proceeded to collect all duties upon goods arriving in the port, compelling the merchants to pay them at the point of the bayonet. Upon the government defeating the rebels and driving *them* out of the city, they, in their turn, demanded the re-payment of the duties which had been forcibly taken by the rebels, and in every instance succeeded in collecting them, and this, too, in the face of hav-ing left the city entirely without protection. One firm alone was victimized during our stay to the tune of over $11,000. There is no doubt that the revolutions are very frequently brought about by some of the foreign residents, who, having large con-signments of goods to arrive, look out for some am-bitious and unprincipled man, willing to lend his name to a *pronunciamento*, and proclaim a new gov-ernment. During the excitement the goods are passed at the custom-house, by order of the parties in power, free of duty, *pretismos* or forced loans are levied upon those who are best able to pay, and so the system of wholesale robbery goes on. In these forced loans the government forces are just as bad or worse than the rebels, for I learn, from the most reliable source, that out of $240,000 paid by the great house of Echeguron Brothers for forced loans during the past nine years, only $37,000 have been paid to the rebel forces. These constant revolu-tions have, as every one knows, been the curse of

Mexico, have degraded her people, stopped the path of progress, and rendered life and property fearfully insecure.   Even during our stay in Mazatlan, two young men of great promise, sons of an old American gentleman whose name and history are well known to me, were cut to pieces within twelve miles of the city, in consequence of some land disputes, and the consul was requested by the bereaved father to make no complaint to his government, or otherwise cause the outrage to become public, as in that case they would murder him!   I am fully convinced that only a very small proportion of the crimes perpetrated upon the foreign residents of Mexico find their way into our newspapers, and the frequency of the little wooden crosses upon the roadsides and in the fields, each one erected to commemorate some violent death, and to ask a prayer for the victim from the passers by, is a sufficient evidence of the lawlessness of the people, and of the small importance they attach to the crime of shedding their fellows' blood!

In Mexico, it seems to me that the principle of justice is unknown, and that might is everywhere superior to right, the motto of all being, " That they should take who have the power, and they should keep who can."

No man now cares to possess himself of a home, for he knows not how soon it might be forcibly taken from him, and he himself thrown upon the world a ruined and broken man. Mines of almost

fabulous wealth, too, lie unworked in the interior
of the country, from the same cause; those in
the hands of foreigners being always defended by
a large force of men, and then not to be regarded
as within the pale of safety.   The claims of
American citizens alone against the Mexican Government for property destroyed, houses ransacked,
operatives murdered, live stock carried off, and
other outrages during the past nine years, amount
in the aggregate to over sixteen millions of
dollars; depositions testifying to these facts, of
the fullest and most complete character, from upwards of a hundred persons, having been collected
by General Adams, the commissioner sent from
Washington to investigate the claims, these depositions being in themselves of such a remarkable
character as to read like a romance of the Middle Ages.   General Adams, in the performance
of his duties, underwent much suffering, and braved
many dangers, riding for hundreds of miles over
roads on which one false step of the mule might
precipitate him and his rider thousands of feet be-
low, and passing without a guard through districts
well known to be infested by bandits of the most
cruel and bloodthirsty nature.   Seeing the worst
and the best side of the Mexican character, he is
enabled to present to his government a fair statement of the case at issue, and to hasten on a better
state of protection for the foreign residents of Mexico than has hitherto been accorded to them.   If the

foreigners who are now settled there chose to
withdraw from the country there is little doubt that
a series of internecine struggles would, in the course
of years, so rapidly diminish the population as to
leave little of the semblance of a nation.

In 1821, when they threw off the Spanish yoke,
the Mexicans numbered over fifteen millions; to-
day the estimate comes under eight millions; inclu-
sive of the large foreign element which has since
that time been introduced. With this terrible de-
crease in the population she presents the melancholy spectacle of a nation fast falling to decay,
her approaching dissolution brought chiefly about
by the ambition and greed of her higher classes,
who should have been the examples and upholders
of a better state of things. The great anaconda of
the North, as some of her writers are pleased to
call the United States, advances slowly upon her
with open jaws; the future of Mexico is plainly
written in the coming time, and her destiny clearly
and legibly foreshadowed. In the common benefit
of our common humanity, let us pray that that time
may soon approach, and that the garden of the
North American Continent may, under a more enlightened government, be made to produce that
bounteous fruit with which it is so capable to bless
and benefit the world !

It is rarely that a month passes without some part
or other of Mexico being in a state of revolution,
and during our visit scenes of blood and rapine were

being enacted in the Canton of Tepic, only about one hundred and fifty miles from Mazatlan, which were of a nature to make the cheek pale and the frame shudder. Manuel Lozada, "General and Natural Chief of the District of Tepic," as he styles himself, had for years past been the terror of the district in which he rules with despotic sway, and had hitherto defeated all attempts of the government to dislodge him. The life of this man is full of such terrible incidents, that the relation of them sounds almost incredible; nevertheless, hundreds of witnesses, many of whom have personally suffered from his cruelty, can bear ample testimony to their truth. He is a full-blooded Indian, and one of the most degraded monsters that ever blotted the page of history, ancient or modern. He was born near Tepic, somewhere about 1824; he is therefore about fifty years of age, and for the earlier years of his life worked as muleteer and laborer on a ranch in the neighborhood. He early in life gave evidence of his cruel and bloodthirsty nature. A man named Morales, passing his mother's hut one day, asked for water, which for some reason or other was refused by the inhospitable Indian, on which Morales applied to her an opprobrious epithet, and rode away. Lozada, then a boy of about eighteen years of age, being apprised of this, swore to have his revenge. Enlisting the services of three companions, he followed Morales for two days, until they came upon his track, when having seized him, they killed his horse, tied him to a tree, cut the skin from the soles of his feet, and compelled him to walk in this condition for several miles, until exhausted nature forbade his proceeding further. They then robbed him of all he possessed, and literally cut him to pieces. Upon this atrocious act being known, an attempt to arrest Lozada was made by the authorities, but he escaped with a few followers to the mountains, the passes and fastnesses of which were well known to him, and amidst which he defied pursuit. Here for several years he held sole possession; and being reinforced by every desperado who could escape the clutches of the loosely administered laws, until his party was upwards of two thousand strong, they made constant raids in every direction, until the very name of Lozada was a sound at which the bravest quailed. Villages burned, churches and dwellings ransacked, men robbed and murdered, and women outraged, were almost daily occurrences, and all efforts to dislodge him proved of no avail. Thousands of dollars were offered for his capture, alive or dead, but without effect; for although he several times descended from the mountains and placed Tepic under contribution, he always managed to carry himself out of the reach of the military, and make good his retreat to the wild and rocky defiles where none dare follow him.

This reign of terror continued for some years, until about 1860. When the Church party came into power, they invited Lozada from his mountains, and in pursuance of their wishes he came to Tepic, proclaimed himself as its governor, professed repentance of his crimes, was baptized by the head of the Church, carried in a grand procession through the streets, and at last canonized as a saint, his festal day being to this very time most rigidly celebrated in Tepic. After this, he suppressed all outrages throughout his district, taking and holding to himself the power to punish crime, and allowing no one to injure another even in self-defence, hanging or shooting any of his followers for the most trifling theft, and utterly abolishing highway robberies and other crimes until then so rife around him. Beyond his province, however, his band of ruffians continued uninterruptedly their reign of blood, without interference from their chief; but it is only just to Lozada to say, that since his so-called conversion, he has made the district of Tepic the most tranquil in the whole of Mexico, and perfectly safe for travellers and others, who could journey through any part of his territory with the utmost safety. His own cruel nature, however, has found vent in the most terrible and disgusting crimes. He caused his wife and mother to be shot before his eyes in the court-yard of his own house, the one for supposed infidelity to him, and the other for concealing her knowledge of it. He surrounded a village of poor people who had offended him, with a troop of soldiers, drove the inhabitants, numbering some one hundred souls, men, women, and children, into their huts, mostly made of branches of the cocoa trees, set fire to them, and roasted the poor wretches alive. A Mr. Chase, an American gentleman, owner of a large tobacco factory near Tepic, once spoke his mind, in the principal hotel of the place, with reference to Lozada's doings, and that very night, on his way home, was seized, thrown into prison, and literally chopped to pieces within a few hours after his honest, but perhaps imprudent, words had been spoken. These are but a few instances of those related to me by gentlemen of credibility, on whose word I could fully rely. I dare not here mention many other still more revolting deeds laid to this monster's charge. With such rulers as this what must be the state of Mexico? And yet, because "there is coin in it," Lozada is to-day upheld by a powerful party, some English and Americans, I blush to say it, being numbered among his political supporters.

Lozada is a man of low stature, with heavy brows and long black hair, and keeps his eyes constantly on the ground. He is never known to look a man in the face, his own being almost concealed by a heavy black sombrero which he wears low down upon his forehead. The crafty wretch has always steadfastly refused to have his portrait taken, though many stratagems have been resorted to to obtain it. A photographer recently hired a house opposite to Lozada's quarters in Tepic, cut a hole through his shutter, and fixed his camera exactly opposite the balcony on which the general was accustomed to walk. Our friend thought every thing was all right, and that the coveted portrait was now a thing of certainty, but Lozada, with the inherent keenness of his race, noticed the change in the shutter, caused the artist to be arrested, and gave him three hours to quit Tepic. I need not say that there was one photographer less in that city on the following morning. This man is immensely wealthy, his money in English banks alone amounting, it is said, to over four millions of dollars ; and by his money and the prestige which attaches to his name, he is enabled to surround himself with an army which numbers some 15,000 strong, and thus to form a powerful antagonist to the government, who will have considerable difficulty to deprive him of his power.

His natural enemy is General Ramon Corona, one of the most intelligent, honest, and patriotic men in Mexico, who, when at the head of his army, never goes better clad than his soldiers, and who, upon a handsome saddle of the value of $500 being given to him in Colima, sold it, and divided the proceeds among his half-famishing troops. Corona is a young man, full of courage and enthusiasm, and has several times put Lozada to a hard push, but the Indian's superior strength has always stood him in stead, and he has invariably remained master of the situation. He appears to bear a charmed life, as he has been lanced twice, shot through and through, stabbed several times, and lately had his right hand shattered and his eye blown out by the explosion of a fuse of giant powder which some one had placed near his person in the hope of getting rid of him. I was informed, however, by a refugee from Tepic, who came to Mazatlan only a few days before I left it, and who fled for safety to that city, that Lozada's earthly career is fast drawing to a close. He is passionately fond of liquor, and his drinking propensities have of late made such inroads upon his constitution, that his death may speedily he looked for. Should this event soon happen, drunkenness will have done the only good thing it ever did in the world's history, and many persons in Mexico will be enabled to say in all sincerity of heart, " Thank God for whiskey."

The revolution then raging in Tepic was the chief topic of excitement at the time of our arrival in Mazatlan, and rumors of a most alarming character were daily reaching us, while crowds of people were arriving constantly, having been driven from their homes by Lozada's troops, or by the fear of what might happen. The people of Mazatlan themselves scare terribly at the thought that Lozada, if he succeed in defeating the government forces, will one day take possession of their city, an operation not at all difficult of accomplishment, as the whole force of soldiery in Mazatlan does not exceed five hundred men, while the entire army of the State of Sinaloa does not reach eight hundred. Those, however, who are best informed on the subject seem to think that he has enough to do to defend his own territory and to keep the forces of the government from occupying Tepic. I see by the latest telegraphic reports, that he has threatened to burn this city, the most beautiful and elegantly built town in the west of Mexico! Our hotel seemed to be a wonderful receptacle of all the rumors which were flying about and disturbing the peace of the people, and one little Frenchman in particular used to choose the hour in which we sat down to our dinner, to rush in and destroy our appetite by his each day more horrible news! He always made a rush into the piazza with an open copy of a telegram in his hand, and running his hands through his hair, would gesticulate and strike an attitude with all that earnestness and extravagance of action so peculiar to his nation. I could occasionally catch the words, " Lozada—beware—blood—death!" and such-like soothing sounds; but when he exclaimed, " Mon Dieu!" and fell dramatically into a chair, I thought it was all up with us, and dropping my knife and fork, I rushed to the top of the house in the vain hope of seeing the signal of an approaching steamer, which should bear me away from such sanguinary scenes to my quiet home in San Francisco. That fellow, however, cried "wolf" too often, and we began to look upon him as a blower, and at last paid little attention to his alarms. We felt ourselves pretty safe, for a few weeks at least, and so re-

solved to think no more of revolutions, and make
the best of our stay. We listened to the band
"discoursing eloquent music" in the plaza at night,
and indulged our love of natural history by day,
heedless of the distracting events occurring around
us, and realizing the elegant words of Thomson:

> " The fall of kings,
> The rage of nations, and the crush of states
> Move not the man who, from the world escaped,
> In still retreats and flowery solitudes
> To Nature's voice attends, from month to month
> And day to day, through the revolving year ;
> Admiring sees her in her every shape,
> Feels all the sweet emotions at his heart,
> Takes what she liberal gives, nor thinks of more."

The country immediately surrounding Mazatlan
consists of a series of broken hills at some little distance,—varying from a half mile to two miles—
from each other, and crowned to their summits with
a dense growth of shrubs and small trees. In the
valleys between these hills is found a rich alluvial
loam, highly retentive of moisture, capable of growing crops year after year without the slightest atom
of artificial manure, and cultivated in the most
primitive style of agriculture. The plows used are
heavy wooden affairs, pointed at the end of the
share, which scratch rather than turn the soil, and
which look like the figures we find upon Egyptian
monuments. These are drawn by oxen, which are
yoked by their horns, and driven by a sharp-pointed

stick. Very little land is under cultivation com-
pared to the vast extent of the country; and in
the uncertain condition of the republic and the
muddled condition of all titles to real estate, it is
not likely that, until a material change shall come
about, much improvement can be hoped for. The
cultivated patches are fenced either with the cactus
or with upright poles, about ten feet high, placed
a few inches apart, and tied together with the ten-
drils of a plant allied to the convolvulus, which
grows abundantly at the sea-side. It is not an unusual occurence to find a cultivated clearing hemmed
round on all sides by a dense, impenetrable bush,
which forms a natural fence superior to all others.
Many, in fact most, of the plants are furnished
with long, sharp, and cruel thorns, which interfere
terribly with one's passage among them, and in the
most ruthless manner tear both clothes and flesh.
Mimosas and cassias, with lovely flowers, giving
forth an exquisite scent, become almost repulsive by
their savage armature, and the pain we suffer as we
attempt to force a way through the thick foliage,
robs us of half our pleasure as we contemplate the
wonders of vegetation scattered everywhere around
us. For there is much, very much, to charm the
senses in the botanical glories of this enchanting
land. Though we were in the winter season, when
the trees and shrubs put on any thing but their gayest livery, we found on every hand abundant illus-
trations of the singular plants which grace the State

of Sinaloa. Large, straggling trees, without the semblance of a leaf, would be crowned at their tops with crowded bunches of flowers, lilac, pink, purple, white, red, and yellow being the conspicuous colors. The growth of flowers before the appearance of the leaves is one of the botanical peculiarities most observable among some classes of vegetation, while grand crimson epiphytes and orchids, parasitic upon the limbs of trees, cannot fail to strike the eye of even the most unscientific observer. The branches of the mesquite trees were frequently ornamented with the nests of the so-called "tailor-bird"—which is really a species of oriole (*Icterus pustulatus*)—singularly formed structures, nearly a yard in length, while troops of gorgeous humming-birds of several varieties might be seen piercing the flowers with their slender tongues. The mesquite (*prosopis glandulosa*) produces a very fine, hard, close-grained wood, which is highly valuable for cabinet work and inlaying, and could easily be made a large article of export. At present it is chiefly employed in the making of charcoal, that produced from the mesquite commanding the highest price in the market.

As we leave Mazatlan and advance nearer to the mountains, the timber becomes larger and of greater variety, and many exquisite specimens of ornamental and sweet-scented woods were shown to me as products of the more hilly districts. The species of plants belonging to the genus *Solanum*, of which the tomato and potato are familiar forms, were especially abundant, and a lovely jessamine, with clear white, wax-like flowers, and a most powerful fragrance, was found in every clump of bushes. One of the india-rubber trees also grows abundantly in some of the forests near the city; its dark green, widely spreading foliage being always a conspicuous object. We saw very few of the higher animals; a small species of rabbit, a squirrel, and the armadillo, being the only varieties which came under our notice. Birds, however, were very numerous, both in species and individuals, and I have seen few places in my life which would better reward the labors of an ornithologist than the country around Mazatlan. It was here that the lamented Grayson made his admirable collection, from which were drawn those exquisite plates which will hand his name down to the future in company with Wilson, Audubon, and Gould. Grayson's remains lie peacefully in the cemetery of the city; and as I stood beside his grave, with that feeling of enthusiastic admiration which one lover of nature always feels for his more gifted brother, I grieved that one so eminent should be, even among his own countrymen, so little known. His book on the " Birds of Mexico," as yet without a publisher, is an exhaustive treatise on the species of the region he so thoroughly explored, and is worthy to take rank among the very first scientific productions of the century. The Pioneer Society of California intend to honor the memory of Grayson by one day conveying his dust to San Francisco. I hope they will follow up this work by causing the publication of his book, as by that means they would raise to his memory a monument far more lasting than marble, and one that will endure while science lives.

In my favorite pursuit of entomology I found much, very much, to interest me, and supply me with food for thought and study for many years to come. It may be of some interest for me to state that during our three weeks' stay we collected up-wards of five thousand specimens of natural history objects, many of which may possibly turn out to be new to science. We searched the woods for plants and insects, and the sea-shore for shells, star-fishes, crabs, and the many other curious forms of marine life, and each day found something strange to us, on which to feast our eyes and to furnish us with materials for investigation at a future day.

We saw but few noxious creatures of any kind, scorpions being certainly the most abundant, and attaining a considerable size. Snakes are very rare, and near the city almost entirely unknown. Ants are numerous, but more remarkable for their beauty than for any distinctive properties. The little leaf-cutting species (*Œcodoma cephalotes*), so at-tractive and at the same time so destructive in Texas and Arizona, are also remarkably abundant in Mazatlan, and nearly every day we came across one of their colonies. These industrious insects line their nests with the leaves and berries of trees, and they wander off an immense distance from their homes in search of their leafy stores. Sometimes for several hundred yards they may be traced along a beaten path, marching in double file, one bearing portions of leaves about half the size of a postage stamp, and the other, having delivered their burden at the nest, returning to the tree for more. In this way they march over sticks and stones, rarely turning out of their way for any impediment, those on the right-hand track never in any way interfering with their opposite neighbors, but going in the most methodical way about their business, apparently thoroughly intent upon their work. I accidentally trod one day upon one of these columns, destroying, of course, several of the insects, and disturbing the course of the army. The ants bearing leaves still continued their journey, but those with empty jaws immediately cleared the track of their dead comrades, and then went on as if nothing had happened. These remarkable insects brought forcibly to mind Shakespeare's lines—

> " Let every soldier hew him down a bough,
> And bear 't before him."

And so, in this strange city, undisturbed by the noise of cars and fire-engines, in which the columns of a newspaper were to us unknown, where no bootblacks or peddlers ever come, where the rush of business forces itself not upon the mind, and the wheels of life roll steadily and lazily along, our time

passed dreamily away. But the pleasures of the
world come suddenly to an end. The last butterfly
was caught, the last strange plant gathered, the last
shell carefully cleaned and put away, when the red
flag on the signal staff announced the coming of a
steamer, and told us that the hour of our departure
had come. That evening, with

"A feeling of sadness and longing
That is not akin to pain,"

we bade adieu to Mazatlan in the darkness, and were
soon once more upon "the deep blue sea," thread-
ing our mysterious way over its ever-restless, ever-
solemn depths.

NOTE.—I must ask my readers to remember
that eight years have elapsed since the foregoing
paper was written, and that during that time many
and important changes have occurred in the history
and manners of Mazatlan. An excellent hotel is
now in course of erection; the abuses in the custom-
house and pilot department have been greatly miti-
gated; the tyrant Lozada has passed to his account; the telegraph is in admirable working order;
and the fruitful valleys of Sinaloa will soon be penetrated by that grand pioneer of civilization, the rail-
road. With such changes in the social condition of
a country come better impulses in the minds of its
people, and it is to be hoped that many of the ob-

stacles to the progress of Mexico which recently existed are swept away, and that she may soon take the place among the nations of the earth to which the possession of a glorious country, a fertile soil, and an almost perfect climate, eminently entitle her.

IRON

AND ITS RELATION TO CIVILIZATION.

An address delivered at the annual opening of the Mechanics' Fair, San Francisco, August 8, 1876.

THE field of thought covered by the title I have chosen for my address is a mighty one, far too vast for the contemplation of an hour, and only on the present occasion to be regarded as the opening of the volume, leaving the wealth of its pages untouched and unexplored. It is one of the contradictions of our imperfect nature, that those objects which are always present with us, and which become as it were a part of our every-day existence, receive too little consideration at our hands. We take them as our right, and utterly unconscious of that spirit of gratitude which should fill our souls at the knowledge of the countless blessings which are ours unsought, we pause not to consider whence they come, how important they may be to our daily wants, or how great the loss we should sustain by their withdrawal from our possession. And iron is one of these, iron—that common metal with which we are all so familiar, with the use of which in some form or other we hourly come in contact, of whose chemical constituents we now know much, whose formation and geologic conditions have been made clear by the light of modern science, but whose discovery by man, and his first application of the metal to the uses of his life, are all but a sealed book to us, the smallest streaks of light alone breaking in upon us to relieve the darkness of our search. Far off in that remote period in which history is utterly lost, and even tradition becomes merged in the gloom of obscurity, we may imagine some dusky savage starting with delight and wonder as he views the sparkling crystals of the heavy lump of stone beneath his feet, of the composition of which he knew nothing, but which in after ages was destined to be the greatest "boon to mortals given," the grand handmaid of progressive civilization, and the all but indestructible basis of the noblest works which ever emanated from the genius of mankind. How the first crude worker in iron conceived the idea of reducing that coarse, heavy mass into a malleable form, rendering it plastic and obedient to the skill of his hands, we know not; here the curtain falls upon our ken, and imagination, unaided by positive knowledge, can alone assist us. Owing, however, to the difficulty which exists in reducing it from its ores, its extreme hardness, and the want of discrimination as to which variety of ore would be the most productive, it would appear that iron was by no means the first metal whose use was learned by our progenitors; doubtless yielding in this respect, to lead, silver, and copper. But still in this statement, we are wandering into the realms of speculation. The condition of man in his earlier stages of existence was probably as different in all its general characters as our own may be from that of the inhabitants of Jupiter or Saturn, and the only certainty we can lean upon is that, the metal once found, its uses gradually became known; the first purposes to which it was applied being, probably, the fabrication of weapons of the chase or of war. These far-off times are shrouded in mystery, but as we stand awhile upon the mountains of thought, far removed from the petty vexations of life, and contemplate the stir which everywhere around us has proceeded with the most ceaseless activity, we see written as the eternal law of Providence, a progressive change from a lower to a higher form of existence, and recognize in every department of our being, examples of this progress working ever upward and onward to a grand purpose—a purpose as yet unfulfilled, but expanding day by day, and hour by hour, nearer and ever nearer to that perfection which, though never absolutely reached, is, in the very nature of things, one day compelled to burst into the open sky of peace, of freedom, and of love. And so, as the geologist, by the aid of physical facts, can trace the growth of worlds and assign to each created thing his place and period in the vast scale of creation, from the azoic age, devoid, as the name implies, of the smallest trace of life, up to that marvellous epoch when the earth echoed with the tread of man,—so can we understand how that mighty being

    " By slow degrees, by more and more,"

improved in growth and culture, and gave evidence, even in those barbaric days, of a civilization yet to be, a civilization still unseen, but as perfect and as certain as is the form of the flower within the un-opened beauty of the bud. And as he grew stronger and stronger, gaining hourly in intelligence, and in each century of his existence removing himself fur-ther and further from the brute condition of his primal form, fulfilling that eternal law of outgrowth which shines with untiring brilliancy upon all the handiworks of God, his wants necessarily became more and more numerous, the products of earth were searched and tested to satisfy his desires, and every object which could by any means aid those wants, was greedily seized, and forced into the army of their supply. Among these iron undoubtedly held a foremost place; and though we can assign no positive period as the date of its first manufacture, the researches of Sir John Lubbock and others have marked its existence among the lacustrine dwellings of Switzerland, away back in those prehistoric times when man had no records, and has left no trace of his existence beyond the buried relics of his prim-itive homes; while, descending the stream of more approximate history, we find that Homer, who is supposed to have lived in the ninth century before Christ, is accredited in Pope's translation of the Iliad and the Odyssey with many allusions to this metal. In the latter poem, Minerva, under the guise of "Mentes, the monarch of the Taphian land," while explaining to Telemachus the reason of her visit to Ithaca, says:

> " Freighted with iron from my native land,
> I steer my voyage to the Brutian strand,
> To gain by commerce from the labor'd mass
> A just proportion of refulgent brass."

These facts would tend to show a greater antiquity for the use of iron than has usually been assigned to it; and explorations made of late years in the great Pyramid of Cheops, have brought to light some wedges of iron firmly embedded in the crevices of the enormous blocks of stone of which those structures are composed, which could not have been manufactured, according to the best Egyptian scholars, subsequent to 3000 B.C., while in the buried cities of Asia and America, iron implements of various kinds, and ornamental designs in the same metal, have been frequently discovered. But it is from that grand storehouse of knowledge which, however degenerated to-day, has been the birth-place of many of our most treasured discoveries, from the

> " Rich Orient, studded with her gems,"

that the first historical records of the uses of iron

came to us, carrying us down the mighty river of time to the more familiar period of the Greek and Roman dynasties, and it is from about three hundred years previous to the Christian era that our really reliable information comes; the Romans, then the masters of the world, being probably the first to perceive the malleable properties of the metal, and to apply it to many uses before unknown. It is certain that the rich mines of the Island of Elba were worked by them upwards of 2,500 years ago, while we learn from the Commentaries of Cæsar that on his invasion of Britain the spears and lances of the inhabitants of that island were either wholly made or tipped with iron, and during the occupation of Britain by Julius and his successors, the rich mines of the Forest of Dean, in Gloucestershire, were constantly worked by the Romans, numberless cinder heaps in that grand old domain still remaining to mark the rude efforts of the conquerors to extract the coveted metal from its rebellious ore. Over many of these cinder heaps, now covered with rich soil, the product of disintegration and decomposition in the past centuries, I have often wandered as a boy, and gathered lovely flowers which grew up in the crevices of these singular remains; the cinder heaps of Dean Forest being spots well known by every naturalist who has visited that region, in winter producing many rare and curious fungi, and in summer equally rare flowering plants, which, in their turn, were visited by insects elsewhere but seldom seen. The furnaces used by these people in smelting the ore are, in many cases, still in existence, being always erected on the top of some eminence, so as to obtain the greatest force of the wind. Charcoal was used for the fires, and it is not difficult in some places to trace the remains of charcoal pits—nay, even of the very trees cut down for the purpose of being converted into fuel. "The processes of extracting the iron were, however, naturally very rude and imperfect, and left so much iron in the cinders, that several of the heaps in the Forest of Dean furnished the chief supply of ore to twenty furnaces for upwards of two hundred years."

From the time of the Romans the workmanship in iron gradually improved, and its use spread over Europe and Asia; large deposits of ore being discovered in Sweden, Russia, Siberia, Persia, Italy, France, and England. The last-named country now produces the bulk of this metal; one bed, in the northeast of Yorkshire, yielding for several years no less than the enormous amount of four hundred thousand tons per annum, while some mines in the county of Cumberland gave, in 1861, the almost incredible result of one million tons. Next to England in point of production stands the United States, though very much that is used is still imported from Europe. There is good reason to hope that, in a few years, by increased facilities, and by the exercise of enterprise and capital, the iron mines of North America will take the lead of all the world, and in their turn supply much of the demand from the older countries across the Atlantic. The early settlers of this country, though soon becoming acquainted with the existence of metalliferous deposits, could not make them a special object of their search, as the beds of ore with which they were enabled to become acquainted were, for the most part, far removed, in those days, from their settlements, and were known chiefly to the Indians, who manifested a hostile feeling to the invaders of their soil. It was not until the year 1702 that a furnace for the purpose of smelting iron was erected in Plymouth County, Mass., being followed a few years later by such other enterprises in Rhode Island and Maryland. The pig-iron thus produced was chiefly exported to Great Britain, where it was admitted free of duty, manufactured articles of iron and steel being returned in its stead. In 1771, the shipment of iron from this country to Great Britain amounted to 7,525 tons, the exportation ceasing with the War of Independence, one hundred years ago.

I am not here to-day to speak to you of your marvellous advances in every department of economy which tends to the permanence of your social progress, since that eventful period of American history in which an oppressed people rose to vindicate their rights, and to trample beneath their liberated feet the shackles which had so long bound them; but I may respectfully, as an Englishman, ask you, natives of this vast and ever-advancing country, to believe that, in common with myself, there are thousands in your mother-land to-day who hail your " Declaration of Independence" as the dawn of a new era of freedom, not for yourselves alone, but for all who have felt the heel of the tyrant, and who crown your glorious work, in this centennial year, with the thanksgiving and the blessing which ever spring from the depths of warm and sympathizing souls. And it is good to remark in this connection, that that very Declaration had in view, in one of its clauses, the grievances which the early settlers experienced in the harsh measures adopted by Great Britain to prohibit the erection of furnaces for the smelting of metals, the mother-country having passed an act denouncing all such erections as " nuisances," fearing that the growth of such manufactories would tend to lessen her hold upon her transatlantic territory. But, happily, this overbearing tyranny is at an end, and by a tremendous bound, rather than by gradual growth, the Union has become the second in importance as an iron-producing country, and this in the short space of a single century.

I find it stated in Gray's " Physical Atlas," that " after the close of the war, the chief supplies were again furnished by Great Britain, from the lack in the United States of the capital necessary for the successful prosecution of the business. The natural advantages possessed by Great Britain, powerfully co-operated with her legislation, and as her rich deposits of iron and coal were in close juxtaposition and in localities not far removed from the coast, the iron interest became so fully established that no nation accessible to her ships could successfully engage in the same pursuit, until by following her example its own mines and resources could be fully developed." In 1810 the amount of pig-iron produced in the United States was 54,000 tons; in 1828 this had increased to 130,000 tons; in 1842, to 240,-000 tons; and in 1870, to the enormous result of 2,052,881 tons—this vast quantity being the product of 3,210,918 tons of iron ore. It may be well for me to add that fully one half of this was mined in the State of Pennsylvania alone; though large deposits of ore exist in Ohio, New York, Missouri, and Michigan—in fact, there are no States in the Union, with the exception of Florida, Texas, and Louisiana, which do not contribute their quota to this priceless branch of industry.

Year by year the yield of iron in the United States, as well as in Europe, is constantly increasing, and from the most reliable statistics at my command, the total product of the year 1874 amounted, in round numbers, to about nine millions of tons, the value of which, taking the average price of pig-iron at that time, was not less than two hundred millions of dollars. The mind almost staggers under these tremendous figures, and did we not know how universal was the use of this metal, we should hesitate to accept such statements. But the purposes to which it is applied in our social economy are all but infinite, and as civilization advances with her giant strides, "iron, more iron," is the cry forever upon her lips, as the grandest need of her progressive path.

It is away from my present purpose to talk to you of the chemical composition of iron. I would not if I could, and I could not if I would; but it may be well for me to state that iron is never in a state of nature found absolutely pure, but exists in combination with other substances, forming oxides, carbonates, phosphates, silicates, and iodides of iron, which are again subdivided into various specific metallic forms and compounds. Probably the richest of all known ores, containing, I believe, nearly seventy-three per cent. of pure iron, is that technically known as the black oxide, a variety for which Sweden is especially famous, the metal produced from it being generally esteemed the best in Europe. The mines of Dannemora, in Sweden, have been constantly worked since the 15th century, while large deposits of this variety (known also as magnetic iron) are found in the Ural Mountains of Russia, and in this country, in Canada, New Jersey, Pennsylvania, and Virginia. "The rock formations in which magnetic iron ore occurs contain no coal, hence it is almost always smelted with wood-charcoal, which, as it contains no sulphur, is one great cause of the superiority of the iron produced from it."

With regard to the process of smelting, I find on the authority of "Chambers's Cyclopedia," that "charcoal was constantly used for this purpose up to 1618,

when Lord Dudley introduced the use of coal; but
the iron-masters being unanimously opposed to the
change, Dudley's improvement died with him, and
was not re-introduced until 1713, when Abraham
Derby employed it in his furnaces at Coalbrook
Dale. About 1750 the introduction of coke gave
renewed vigor to the iron trade, and then followed
in rapid succession those improvements in its manufacture which give to the history of iron all the
interest of a romance. The steam-engine of Watt;
the process of puddling and rolling invented by
Henry Cort, in 1784; the employment of the hot
blast by Neilson, of Glasgow, in 1830; and the well-
known Bessemer process of later days, were grand
discoveries in this branch of industry, and worthy
pioneers of the more extended knowledge of the
reduction and utilization of the metal which, year
by year, is made to dawn upon the horizon of mechanical science.

Indeed, the energy and intelligence bestowed
upon the subject of iron throughout the world, are
in themselves sufficient to prove its extreme importance to the race, did not its multifarious uses come
hourly beneath our notice, and testify to its existence as a necessity of our being. Who can over-
value its worth? Who can attempt to sum up the
comforts we derive, the blessings we enjoy, from a
knowledge of its uses and its power? The miles
on miles of railways which stretch themselves like
a net-work over the surface of our planet, binding

continents together in a bond of fellowship, and linking distant nations hand to hand, would have no existence, but for iron; the pumps which draw the sparkling water for us from the depths of the earth; the pipes which convey it from distant reservoirs for our cities' use; the fleets of white-winged ships which stud our seas, like messengers of love, carrying blessings from one land to another, exchanging the fruits of the earth, and cementing the whole world in one compact and universal brotherhood; the grand and complicated machines which fill your courts to-day, and attract the attention and move the wonder even of mechanical minds; the lofty structures which rise around us on every hand, sublimely reaching up to heaven as if in mute but earnest praise to the grand creative Mind whence all has sprung, attest in trumpet tones the precious boon which iron has become to man—the most important want and blessing of his race.

Turn where we will, its worth is seen; examine where we may, its power and its uses are experienced and known. There is no position in life, no rank in society, which is independent of its assistance. Not only in those mighty works, which assert man's claim to the gratitude of coming ages, but in the minor details of our daily life, in all the countless relations which go to make up the sum and comfort of our being, the value of this marvellous product is enforced upon our attention.

The surgeon's instruments, and the bridge which

spans a cataract; the dainty needle, and the hammer which can crush a ton; the scythe of the mower, and the lever which can stir a palace ; the fearful war-guns before whose fire whole armies sink as puppets, and the wire which cages the imprisoned bird; the light-houses which protect our coasts, throwing their beacon lights far across the deep as the wanderer's warning and his sign, and the pen which writes our messages of love ; the delicate mechanism which guides the movements of our watch, and the stupen-dous columns which lift themselves far up into the eternal and bare their brows to God,—these are but a few of the varied purposes to which it is applied, and for which it claims our recognition and regard! And let us ever remember, that for it no substitute can be offered—no metal known to us can take the place of iron in its controlling and multifarious uses. For gold, silver, copper, lead, or tin, something may be found to supply the place ; for iron, nothing !

It is terrible to contemplate the utter blank which the world would become, if it were possible that by some sudden convulsion it could be withdrawn from us and banished from the earth. As if by the touch of a magician's wand, a desolation, vast and awful, to which the most fearful earthquake that ever devastated the world would be but as the falling of a house of cards, the plaything of a child, would come upon us,—a desolation so stupendous and so crushing in its immensity as to suggest the day foretold by the prophet, "a day of darkness

and of gloominess, a day of clouds and of thick
darkness,"—a desolation which would send our planet
with its thirteen hundred millions of souls drifting
backward and ever backward to her primitive condition, the intelligence of her inhabitants fading
with the lapse of the ages, and her surface becoming
gradually unfitted for the abode of man !

The mind can hardly realize the change—the
paralysis of all endeavor, the destruction of the
mighty aids to labor, the uprooting of all social and
business institutions, and the total annihilation of
commerce in all its forms which would follow such a
vast and overwhelming catastrophe ! Our grandest
edifices would crumble into dust ; our noble
ships would become shapeless masses, and go
down rotting to the sea's extremest depths ; our
telegraph would no longer waft its messages with
lightning speed, putting " its girdle round about the
earth"; our mighty engines, which now with almost
a living voice proclaim themselves the emperors of
force and power, which carry us with such rapidity
from place to place, making the once unknown corners of the earth but pleasant visiting spots for a
summer tour, would pass forever from our sight ;
our printing-press would cease its holy labor ; our
fields would become choked with weeds, and the
furrows of the plough be known no more ! The
civilization of which we now so· worthily boast
would have run its course, would lapse into the
barbarism out of which it sprung, and

" Like an unsubstantial pageant faded,
  Leave not a rack behind ! "

This may be a melancholy picture, but it by no
means exaggerates the endless evils we should suffer,
could the iron of the earth be at once eliminated
from its products; and the contemplation of such an
appalling wreck should at least help us to be grateful for so powerful an adjunct to our social wants.
And looking down the vista of the coming years, do
we not, with our more interior vision, see the possibility of a still wider application to the cravings of
a succeeding race, than any we have known ? Does
not the daily growth of the arts and sciences which
occupy man's attention to-day, and the cultivation
of which adds hourly to his refinement, and brings
his nature nearer and ever nearer to the Divine,—
does not this suggest the existence of uses for this
metal even greater than those we already know—
uses as yet but dimly seen, even by the speculative
and far-seeing mind ? Perhaps we are but yet upon
the threshold of the temple, and the secrets beyond
the vestibule may yet be hidden from our gaze. In
the more refined arts of life—in engraving, in pho-
tography, in the polishing of various substances, in
the cutting of glass, and in the structure of ornamental designs, our knowledge may be fairly said to
be in its infancy; and turning from the peaceful
and purifying arts of life, to considerations of an
opposite character, do we not with a thought perceive how, of late years, at least within our present

century, iron has been employed by man to meet
one of the exigencies of his nature, in the construction of those vast and fearful implements of war,
which are among the most striking features of our
age? The iron-clad ships which, in their present
and more perfected form, had their origin in
America, and which to the number of nearly four
hundred, with the aggregate equipment of over three
thousand guns, are now employed by all the warlike
nations of the globe, are due to the existence of
iron. The perfect immunity of these vessels to the
discharges of the cannon in vogue among our fathers,
suggested heavier artillery, and more powerful guns
were needed to penetrate the armor of this mighty
fleet. Those of modern times have attained such
sizes and such power, that we stand aghast at the
marvellous amount of ingenuity and constructive
genius which men have devoted to the destruction
of each other, and wonder if that glorious period
spoken of by Tennyson—

" When the war drum throbbed no longer, and the battle flags were
      furled
  In the Parliament of man, the Federation of the world "—

lives but in a poet's dream. The guns made by
Krupp, of Prussia, who was one of the pioneers of
this branch of industry, challenge our admiration, at
the same time that they excite our awe.

One of these stupendous weapons, made for the
Russian government in 1868, had a total weight of
fifty tons, the diameter of the bore being fourteen

inches, and the length of the barrel two hundred
and ten inches.   This gun would carry a shot weighing one thousand two hundred and twelve pounds,
the propulsion of which would require a charge of
not less than one hundred and fifteen pounds of
powder.   The price of this gun, with its carriage
and turn-table complete, amounted to one hundred
and fifty thousand dollars of our currency; the time
occupied in its construction being sixteen months of
unremitted labor.   How terrible the expenditure of
all this skill and power for the one purpose of destruction!   But as in the physical world we see that
earthquakes, hurricanes, and volcanoes subserve a
useful purpose, and prepare the earth for the culture
and the use of man, so is it held by many thinking
and philanthropic minds, that with the improvement
of our weapons of war, the era of peace will the more
speedily come,—that era of which Elihu Burritt, the
learned worker in iron, who was " transplanted from
the anvil to the editor's chair, by the genius of
machinery," triumphantly says :   " War shall die,
and all things that love the face of man and the
face of nature, that love to look up into the pure
and peaceful sky, that commune with the silent
harmonies of the great creation, and listen to the
music of unreasoning things,—all these shall fill the
heavens with one grand jubilate that the great can-
nibal is dead!"   But however this may be, certain
is it, that through these mighty engines of destruction the strife of nations will no longer be decided

in close contact upon the blood-stained deep, or on the crowded battle field. " The sword may indeed be turned into a ploughshare and the spear into a pruning-hook," but the horrors of war will be rendered more shortlived, even if more devastating and more decisive, in their operation; and while we sorrow over the deadly feuds which agonize our race, let us remember that the destinies of nations are in wiser hands than ours, and that we, in our impotence, can but look on, wonder, and revere.

I feel that I have already detained you too long, but I must, before I conclude, say a few words as to the existence upon our own coast of the metal we have had under consideration, and the probability of its one day becoming an object for the employment of capital. It may be already known to you that in several portions of this State, deposits of iron ore exist, which need only increased enterprise to render them of immense value and importance. In Sierra Valley, near Marysville, and near Colfax, large beds of ironstone have been discovered, and when it is known that, according to a statement recently made in the *Mining and Scientific Press* of this city, " the quantity of iron annually used upon this coast cannot be less than 60,000 tons, worth in the rough, about $3,000,000, and in a manufactured state not less than $10,000,000," it must be allowed that the development of the iron resources of California and the neighboring States is at least worthy of consideration. In Oregon, some excellent mines, producing ore of the very finest quality, have long been profitably worked; and in British Columbia, a whole island in the Gulf of Georgia, known as Texada Island, waits but the energy of a few determined men to give to the world iron ore sufficient to keep employed hundreds of laborers for many decades to come.

The city of San Francisco alone has within its limits no less than forty-seven iron foundries, machine shops, and boiler factories, employing upwards of three thousand hands, expending annually for wages not less than $1,000,000; and yet it is safe to say that not more than two thousand tons of the iron used by these establishments are the product of our own region. It would appear that there is something wrong here, when we consider that the deposit on Texada Island, to which I have just alluded, contains on a rough estimate nearly twelve millions of tons of ore, and that the cry of dear coal and scarcity of wood for the purposes of making charcoal, which may have some weight in California, cannot prevail here, abundance of both coal and wood being close at hand for the purposes of smelting, while nature affords every facility for shipping the result of the enterprise, and conveying it to its market in other lands. Surely it cannot be deemed Utopian to believe that the day is not far distant when this production of a metal in so general demand all over the world will become one of the most attractive industries of our coast, and that we may supply our numerous foundries with the basis of their labor, mined and smelted within the limits of our own boundary.

At the close of the first century of her independent existence, America has no reason to be abashed at her condition among the nations; and when we think that California has hardly completed her first quarter of the same period, we may well be proud of the progress which she displays to-day! States, like children, must have time to grow, and, expanding into maturity, to shake off the weaknesses of their early growth; and if we are now passing through a stage of fast life, too eager for the sudden acquisition of wealth, and neglectful of opportunities which lie within the reach of our hands, the day is not far distant in which we shall cast off the too feverish excitement which surrounds us now, and with more sober judgment, and experience none the less valuable because purchased in the market of failure, direct our energies and our power to the grandest foundations on which the prosperity of a country can be based—the enlightened cultivation of her soil, and the industrious and intelligent development of her mineral treasures!

BUBBLES FROM BOHEMIA.

" The earth hath bubbles as the water hath,
And these are of them."—*Macbeth*.

SHAKESPEARE.

" HIGH JINKS," April 27, 1873.

A LITTLE over three centuries ago, in an obscure town in the midland counties of England, seated on the edge of a silvery river, in the bosom of a lovely country hereafter to be hallowed by the glory of immortal genius, in this memorable month of April, the quiet household of a simple tradesman was made happy by the birth of a son—an incident of small importance in itself, but fraught with wondrous interest when in these later days we look back upon the past, and recognize the influence which that new-born infant has since exercised upon the minds of civilized people throughout the world, and the halo of eternal honor with which by common consent he has been crowned. The pride and glory of the Anglo-Saxon race, by universal opinion placed at the very apex of fame's topmost pinnacle, his works translated into every language, his noble and passionate thoughts taught in every tongue, and his sublime utterances glowing upon every cultivated lip, he stands alone and unapproachable among the world's worthies, as the inspired exponent of whatever is grand in human thought, of whatever is exquisite and tender in human sympathy, and of whatever serves to throw an illuminating radiance upon the more gloomy recesses of man's mysterious and many-sided soul. The solemn depths of abstruse philosophy, the comprehensive domain of moral and social science, and the grand empire of external nature were alike open to his penetrating vision; and while the sounding tread of the advancing army of man's progressive thought found an echo in his soul, he ever and anon turned aside to contemplate the fairer forms around him, and to paint the glories of creation's universe in colors which can never fade, but which derive an added freshness as we view them by the light of that increased culture bestowed upon us by the passage of the years. The details of his personal life are meagre in the extreme; but though we cherish every trifling part connected with his history, so long as his divine works remain with us the incidents of his career are but of little moment, as in the utterance of Shakespeare's name, we pass out of the sphere of life in which he moved when on earth, and associate ourselves with him more by the magnetism of his genius than by the knowledge of how he looked or talked, or what social position he was called upon to fill. That he was kind and gentle in his nature we are well assured; that he was beloved by his friends we have the fullest testimony; and that his large and generous heart found ample gratification in administering to the welfare of others, can be established beyond a question. A hater of injustice and a foe to tyranny; fighting, in a somewhat darkened and

slavish age, the battle of equal rights for all mankind; always upholding the cause of the oppressed,
and fearing not to expose and lay bare to view the
follies and crimes of vicious rulers, he was preëminently a reformer of the most exalted and unselfish
type. The lessons which he everywhere teaches, of
duty to parents, of the love which should pervade
the social circle, of the respect which should be
given to the gentler sex, of the strict honesty of
purpose which should characterize every action of
our lives, the abiding faith which he inculcates, of
reliance on a higher power, and the grand and
solemn truths which he utters as to the immortality
of man's soul, exhibit to us in a most powerful
degree the excellence of his moral nature; and the
grains of gold which he has everywhere scattered
along the highway of life, indicate the unbounded
wealth of his genius and the wondrous fertility of
his mental power.

What subject has he not touched? What theme
has he not exalted? What phase of intellectual
beauty has he not polished and adorned? In saying
of him that " he was not for an age, but for all time,"
his brother poet has but echoed the universal senti-
ment of mankind; for judging Shakespeare's genius
by the light of our modern civilization, we see clearly
how far in advance of his own age were most of the
principles which he inculcates, and how, even with us,
he still points to a higher and more refined state of
society than that which we now enjoy. And as the

centuries roll on, so will the divine principles of his enduring philosophy receive, year by year, a fuller and more extended illustration ; and as they have taught our fellows in the past, so in the time to come, will generation after generation drink in the nectar of their ambrosial truths, and banquet on the feast of holy thoughts and gorgeous combinations which have been so lavishly spread before them. The clouds which gather round and make dim the record of the past, roll away at his mystic touch, and the history of the feudal ages becomes a living, breathing reality—the fanciful realm of the creatures that

> " On the sand, with printless foot,
> Do chase the ebbing Neptune,"

is no longer a freak of the imagination, but by his wizard's wand starts forth into a quick and active world. The varying scenes of life's solemn drama are peopled by veritable beings, who awaken our sympathies, our love, our terror, or our hate, and bind us into a fast communion with their thoughts, their sufferings, and their deeds. We shudder with Lear upon the gloomy heath : we are weary with Touchstone among the groves of Arden ; we weep with Romeo over his Juliet's tomb ; we " suffer love" with Benedick ; and feel with the melancholy Dane " how stale, flat and unprofitable are all the uses of this world."

Shakespeare's creations are flesh and blood, real, tangible, bodily men and women, and their words

are to us as the exalted thoughts of daily life, refined and elevated by contact with a superior condition of being. Nothing which involves the welfare
of the race is too grand for his consideration ; nothing
which the Creator has called into being is too insig-
nificant for the studious contemplation of his mind.
The spirit of prophecy has more than once descended
upon him, and the completion of Puck's girdle round
about the earth was to him a thing of certainty.
In law, he is a lawyer; in statecraft, a statesman ;
in medicine, a wise physician ; in government, a
ruler ; and in the wide and varied field of science, a
careful and acute observer.   He is preëminently a
naturalist, in the broader sense of the term, not the
man of mere technical knowledge, of names and
terms, of dry classification, whose brain is filled with
genera and species, varieties and races, groups and
affinities, but one possessed of that faculty of observation (given but to few) even of the meanest things
—a power of discovering their varied uses, and pointing out their rank and value in the great chain of
nature.   The rocks and woods, the trees and flowers,
the rolling sea, the calm and tempest, the sunbeam
and the dew-drop, the tiny insect and the giants of
the animal world, are alike to him emblems of creative power, and speak to his receptive soul in the
Divine language of his God.

It would be easy to point out very many of the
instances in which Shakespeare has so forcibly
shown his wonderful observation of the many

phenomena of nature, of the winds and storms, of
the influence of the tides, of the strange mystery of
vegetable life, of the " sermons in stones " beneath
our feet, and of those wonderful instincts in the
lower order of creatures which tread so closely
on the heels of reason ; instances which, for clear-
ness of expression, and conciseness of description,
have never been excelled. Who can ever forget
Miranda's picture of the tempest, or Lorenzo's
exquisite " patines of bright gold " ? while the syl-
van scenes of " As You Like It " are redolent
of country perfume, and shed on the heart an
influence of calm and peace. The accuracy of
Shakespeare as an observer is proved by the fidelity
to the times of their appearance, with which Perdita
strings together her wildflowers at the sheep-shear-
ing ; by the " ugly and venomous " toad, now by the
investigations of modern science discovered to emit
an acrid poison ; and by the fact that Huber, who
devoted his whole life to the subject, added but
little to our knowledge, and certainly left no more
perfect description of the habits of the honey-bee,
than that given by Shakespeare in " Henry the V ":

> " So work the bees :
> Creatures that by a rule in nature teach
> The act of order to a peopled kingdom.
> They have a king, and officers of sorts ;
> Where some, like magistrates, correct at home ;
> Others, like merchants, venture trade abroad ;
> Others, like soldiers, armed in their stings,
> Make boot upon the summer's velvet buds ;
> Which pillage they with merry march bring home,

To the tent-royal of their emperor ;
Who, busied in his majesty, surveys
The singing masons building roofs of gold,
The civil citizens kneading up the honey,
The poor mechanic porters crowding in
Their heavy burdens at his narrow gate ;
The sad-eyed justice with his drowsy hum,
Delivering o'er to executors pale
The lazy, yawning drone—"

His knowledge of law was vast and comprehensive ; and one of the most distinguished judges of modern times, the late Lord Campbell, has devoted a volume to an examination of Shakespeare's legal phraseology, the closeness with which he has everywhere followed the technicalities of this somewhat uninviting subject, being as wonderful as it is admirable. His enunciation of the principles of moral philosophy has furnished the groundwork for many an elaborate address, and no essay on the subject can be completed without a reference to him, and a quotation from his writings. In politics, in religion, in the minor duties of life, he stands forward as a teacher and a text, and perhaps the laws which should govern society have received a fuller illustration from him than from all the writers who have ever lived—an illustration all the more forcible, because, clothed in delightful imagery, it takes deep root in men's souls, and by its own inherent power, buds and blossoms into beauty.

Upon the art of which, apart from his literary genius, he was a worthy and conscientious professor, he has shed an undying lustre, and the drama and

Shakespeare are now inseparable, linked together by a chain which time can never destroy, and mutually strengthened by the improving taste of mankind, and by the mastery over ignorance, which belong to the true, the beautiful, and the good. Much as may be said about the decline of the drama, there is not a night in the year on which, in some theatre or other, a play of Shakespeare's is not performed; and the worthy way in which, assisted by the necessary and pleasing adjuncts of scenery and costume, his works have of late years been presented, is in itself sufficient evidence of his value as a teacher, and of the desire on the part of the people to honor themselves by honoring him.

The magnificent mounting of many of Shakespeare's dramas by the enterprise of Macready and Kean, and still later by Mr. Calvert, has become a matter of theatrical history in England, while in your own country Edwin Booth, Lawrence Barrett, and John McCullough have acquired the gayest leaves of their managerial wreaths by the care evinced by them in the production of these immortal creations. It is not too much to say that such men are public benefactors—they familiarize the mind of the spectator with language of the most exalted strain, and teach the history of almost forgotten periods by an appeal to the intelligence through the medium of scenic decoration. Decline of the drama, forsooth! As long as the English language lasts, as long as Shakespeare exists to us, the drama as an art can never decline, and the more frequent production of his plays will educate a race of actors, who will give a more lasting strength to their noble profession, and tend more and more to elevate it to its proper rank among the teachers of our age. By the vast extent and variety of his subjects, the extreme familiarity with all topics on which he has employed his pen, this "myriad-minded man" stands forth to us as the world's wonder; and it is not a matter of surprise that some doubt should exist in the minds of many, as to his sole authorship of the works ascribed to him, and that many theories should have been set up as to their origin. One of these theories will be elaborately and ably presented to you to-night, and a talented argument will be given to you for consideration, to the effect that the dramas which we reverence so much, were the work of Lord Bacon. Without here expressing any opinion upon the subject, I will only say, that "these opinions, if they prove nothing more, prove the exaltation of the object; their contradictions are praise. For, as men differ not about those things within their reach, but only about those above it," so is the nature of Shakespeare's liquid inspiration above our reach, save so far as its golden drops bubble over its chalice "to quench the thirsty lips of the world." I know well how difficult it is to say any thing new of our honored poet. I know how in praising him, we are liable to "gild refined gold;" but in an hour like this, when, with that friendly communion which exists among us, we meet, in that conviviality of soul which he so much enjoyed, to lay our poor offerings upon the altar of his memory, the homage, however weak, must be paid ; the tribute, however unworthy, must be rendered ; the worship, however imperfect, must ascend to the roof-tree of his mighty temple.

According to the universal doom of our common humanity, he has long passed away from earth, but his influence is felt with increasing power day by day, refining and softening all who come within its sphere, by the light of its eternal radiance dissipating the gloomy shadows of life, and casting upon the pathway of many a weary wanderer a gleam of glory which will light with cheerfulness and joy the track of his onward steps.   And

> " If there be, as holy men have deemed
> A land of souls beyond that sable shore,"

surely it is not too much to believe that the beaming gentleness of his nature looks down upon our festal hour, and clothes our night's enjoyment with the unspeakable beauty of his smile.

ADDRESS ON THE OCCASION OF THE REMOVAL OF THE BOHEMIAN CLUB FROM SACRAMENTO STREET TO PINE STREET, DECEMBER, 1876.

The time has come in which, as we lay aside, with a feeling somewhat akin to regret, the old garment that, for many an hour, has shielded us in sunshine and in storm, we must bid adieu to these pleasant rooms which have so long echoed to the sound of merry laughter, to the swell of mysterious and entrancing music, and to the utterance of the many bright thoughts which have had their origin within the compass of their walls. About every parting common to this life of ours, there is some tinge of regret, and surely we may be pardoned if, amid the thoughts which throng upon us at the recollection of all that enjoyment which we have partaken of within this "small domain," a shade of sorrow should steal for a moment over us, as we think that this is the last time we shall ever gather in this place—a place hallowed by many delightful memories,—which will, long after we have quitted it, be haunted in our minds by the spirits of all the good things that have had their birth within its confines, and by the echoes of that innocent mirth which, while giving zest and enjoyment to the hour, has left no sting behind. Five years have not

entirely rolled by since the foundation of this
Society, and it is not too much to say, that in those
five years the progress made by the Bohemian Club
is a fact in which its members may justly take an
honorable pride, for its success has been of such a
nature as to redound to the credit, not only of those
more immediately interested in its welfare, but to
the community among which it was formed, and to
the city which can boast of an organization at once
so powerful and so elevating in its character. The
existence of a true purpose in life, to the attainment
of which the strongest efforts of man's will are
directed, and whose goal is kept steadily before the
mental eye, is the surest incentive to worldly
advancement; and the purpose of this Club, ever
held in view by those who have had the direction
of its affairs, has been one grand cause of its prosperity to-day. That purpose is evidenced in the
many delightful evenings, like the present, which
we have passed together, in which many an original
contribution has been given to music and literature,
well deserving a wider field of recognition and
regard. Within another year, I trust that some of
the best of these will be presented in a permanent
form to the world, so that a visible record may be
offered, if any were needed, that all that passes here
is not "idle jest and useless laughter," but that our
"High Jinks" have been the means of inspiring
many a worthy thought and inculcating many a
useful lesson. Nor is it less a cause for congratula-

tion, that an utter want of selfishness has been exhibited among us, and that what we have had to give has been given without stint to strangers in common with ourselves. Since our organization, not less than one thousand invitations have been issued to visitors from a distance and to residents of the city, and we can at least claim the merit of dispensing what hospitality we have had to offer with no niggardly hand. And it is but fair to add that that feeling has been duly reciprocated, and that most of the distinguished men and women who have visited San Francisco during our Club existence have honored these rooms with their presence and entered warmly and with considerable interest into our doings and our hopes.

Our absent members, too, are winning honors for themselves, and at the same time spreading in far-off lands the beneficial influences of our society. Miller and Stoddard are crowning themselves with literary honors; Randolph Rogers is glorifying himself and his beloved art by new triumphs; and Williamson is earning fame and fortune before a critical London audience. Nor are our own resident artist members to be overlooked, for among them are many names of which any community may well be proud, and their earnest devotion to the studies they have chosen as their own, gives brilliancy to the Association of which they are honored members, and at the same time elevates the people among whom they dwell.

So that, in bursting from the chrysalis state of our past existence, into the more brilliant one of that which is to come, we leave behind us no regrets, but go forward with courage and determination to what seems a bright and pleasant future. I have said, "We leave behind us no regrets"; but is that so? And are no sad memories connected with the hours we have passed here? Alas! alas! A spectre sits at every feast, and the cloud and the sunshine are always near each other! At this moment come crowding upon us recollections of many a comrade who has gone down in the march of life, "whose place is vacant by the hearth," and who has passed onward in his journey

> " To join
> The innumerable caravan which moves
> To that mysterious realm, where each shall take
> His chamber in the silent halls of death."

The list is longer than we like to think, for fourteen of our companions have passed away from earth; and though the very names of some may be unknown to many of you, there are a few who are "familiar in your mouths as household words," and of whom you daily speak with affection and regret. The genial, eccentric, kind-hearted Johns, who left behind him so bright a record of goodness and honesty of heart, that all who knew him loved and respected the strong sincerity of his character; the generous, indefatigable Ralston, whose loss to San Francisco yet wrings the hearts of her people; the grand, self-sacrificing "Caxton," whose genius was only equalled by his tenderness of soul, and whose recognition as a man of letters, though tardy, will be none the less and secure lasting; the cultivated Ross Browne, who went down to his resting-place in the prime of his manhood, carrying with him the regrets of educated minds in every corner of the earth in which the English language is spoken and literature is honored as a teacher of humanity; and "under the sod and the dew" lies the gentle, loving, woman-like heart of Owen Marlowe, whose clinging nature found room for sympathy with every creature with whom he came in contact: all these have wandered with the grim ferryman over the river,

> "Into the land of the departed,
> Into the silent land."

And there is another yet, known only to a very few within the hearing of my voice, who, had he lived, would have been one of the Club's brightest ornaments, as he was one of the most amiable and unselfish of men. I allude to Charles Duquesnay, for a long time editor of the *Courier de San Francisco*, who possessed talents of no common order, but who was one of that large and unappreciated class

> "Whom fortune frowns on,
> Whom authority oft uses and forgets—
> But still their souls are the world's life-blood.
> The men who think,
> Whose weapon is the pen, whose realm the mind;
> I mean not laurelled bards, but daily workers,

Who, like the electric force, unseen, pervade
The sphere they quicken, nameless till they die,
And leaving no memorial but a world
Made better by their lives."

All these, and others less prominent in their varied walks of life, have gone forever from our earthly gaze; but they have left us happy in the recollections of their friendship, recollections of so sweet a nature as to induce us to echo the simple prayer of one of a great master's creations, a prayer uttered at this same festive season :

" Lord, keep my memory green."

I am far from desiring to cast a gloom over this meeting, or to check the flow of merriment which is to-night everywhere around us; but something has whispered to me that we owed a duty at this hour to those dear associates who can be with us bodily no more, and that it was my part of that duty to pay this imperfect tribute to their memory.

And so, as the Romans of old bore with them, in each change of dwelling, the Lares and Penates which had guarded their hearth-stone, and had been the unseen sentinels of their worldly welfare, let us, as we fold down the page which contains the record of our comrades' lives, bear with us from this spot the knowledge of all that was good in them, and remember with gratitude an association which made brighter the pathway of existence, and robbed our daily labor of half its burden, by the knowledge that there were bright and genial souls who shared the weight of the load, and who, with the true heroism which they manifested, "pointed the moral" of our own individual lives.

EDWIN ADAMS.

This admirable actor and warm-hearted man died in November, 1877, and at the next "High Jinks" of the Bohemian Club, of which he was a member, the following was read, the subject chosen for the evening's consideration being "DREAMS"!

Dreams and Dreamland! Magic words, fraught with such sweet and tender mystery! How potent is the spell they weave around our lives! How all-absorbing is the power with which they hold us in their grasp! The many hours of weird uncertainty, of lingering between *this* earth and that all but impenetrable shadow of the world beyond, which is their special realm, are, of our daily life, "a thing apart"; and as the soul returns to its material surroundings, how jarring sometimes is the shock, but how gentle are the recollections of our wanderings in that strange land of wild, unreal realities! The actions of those silent hours go with us through the day, and give a color to the waking world around us.

> " I would recall a vision, which I dreamed—
> Perchance in sleep—for in itself a thought,
> A slumbering thought, is capable of years,
> And curdles a long life into one hour."

The scene is a pleasant New England village, fresh in the calm radiance of the setting sun. The trees are waving their last requiem to the fading rays—the birds are darting toward their downy resting-places, and the busy hum of life, which a few hours before was strong in its mighty activity, dies into the softest murmur, heralding the approach of a silence at once most solemn and profound. The time is one fitted for meditation, and grateful to the thoughtful soul. Beneath the deepening shadows of those mighty oaks, there sits a youth of less than fifteen summers. A sense of deep and earnest thought is in his face, and away across the distant waters his eye looks longingly and with a flash of hope. No pampered child of wealth is he, but one reared in the midst of life's hardest struggles; yet is he fair to look upon, and in his bright and speaking face, and noble brow, may be traced the presence of an intellect above the common range. His thoughts are deep and somewhat mournful, but there is a light in his looks which tells of energy and power, the power which crushes obstacles, and treads obstructions down. The dog which crouches at his feet and gazes wistfully into his companion's eyes, is now scarce noted by him; but in the open book within his hand is seen the subject of his reflection, for on the page I read the words of the master:

> "Our doubts are traitors,
> And make us lose the good we oft might win
> By fearing to attempt."

By the wizard hand of Fancy, the curtain which

shrouded the future from his gaze has been partially withdrawn, and a picture opened to his view, which the fertile fancy of youth presents in fairy hues. He longs to enter the confines of that seemingly celestial realm, and, in the eagerness of his young life, he casts his doubts behind him, and, with the resolution of an ardent soul, goes forth to " do and dare."

The scene is changed!

Beneath the flashing lights of a crowded assembly, with the eyes of the multitude directed toward him, and the sympathies of his fellows drawn by the magnetism of his own nature into closest communion with him, the boy is seen again. There is no trembling, no hesitancy now; fear has given place to anxiety, but the hopeful, earnest spirit is powerful over all! His rich and sympathetic voice sinks deep into the hearts of those around him, and their unsparing plaudits assure him that his struggles will not be in vain, but that the charmed vision which the day-dream of his earlier youth had fashioned for his gaze might yet be realized; that the goal which seemed to him so distant then, might yet be his to win.

Again the scene is changed!

That goal is won! The crudities of boyhood have been left behind, and the man stands forth before his fellow-men, a teacher and a king! A teacher—for he utters the grandest thoughts of grandest minds, with power which elevates while it

entrances; which charms and fascinates, while it
enforces lessons of the highest truth! A king—
for he rules the realm of imagination with a monarch's sway, and receives the homage of admiring
crowds! Perhaps the poetic dreams of his past
have given place to stern realities; perhaps he has
learned that the colors of the fairy picture fade by
near approach—that the tinsel is not so bright as it
once appeared,—but the closer communion with his
kind, which a larger experience has given, has
widened his heart and enlarged his sympathies, until
with a generous and loving soul he takes all mankind into his embrace, and longs to shed the warmth
of his own glorious nature upon all around him. He
loves and is loved by all; his hand is grasped in
cordial friendship by those to whom he comes, and
his path is made bright by the blessings of well-
earned affection. The garlands of an enduring fame
are placed upon his brow, and his step is lightened
by the knowledge that the appreciation which he
longed for and strove so hard to gain, has come to
him in the prime of his manhood. The future is
broad and bright before him, and he looks boldly into the coming years as fraught with promises
of grander triumphs and extended opportunities.
More for others than for himself he seems to live,
and the surroundings of his existence are but the
means of bringing joy to the saddened heart—the
expression of a boundless generosity, which was at
once a giving and a praise!

Another transformation comes !

The loved one is lying low! The strong and well-knit frame is wasted by disease, and the clear and ringing voice is soft and feeble in its tone! The hand so often stretched to aid is all but powerless now, and the bright and flashing eye is gradually parting with its lustre!

But the energy, the unyielding spirit of youth, are there; the cheerfulness of soul is still as strong as ever, and the merry jest and kindly speech yet ring with laughter from the tongue! The sweet and gentle love of woman is near to tend and soothe the sufferer; and men, with hearts made soft by sympathy, look on, and wonder if their friend can die! If love, and hope, and friendship's strongest bonds could have driven the destroyer away, the moment which all dreaded, but which all knew was fast approaching, would have been long postponed, for his departure from amongst us could but be regarded as a loss the world can seldom feel, an infliction which time can but rarely impose! But the finger of the angel had touched him, and gently beckoned him away. Across the dark valley which must one day be travelled by us all, he passed in calmness and in peace, unconscious of the wail of sorrow which announced the completion of his journey! The Godlike spirit of friendship made happy his parting hours, and the loving one who tended his sick couch with the courage of a martyr, has felt the kindliness of heart which he inspired, a slight return only for the good he did for others, and for the many noble deeds which had their spring in the fountains of his own loving and tender nature.

Again a change appears !

A casket strewn with flowers, sweet emblems of affection and of hope, followed by a tearful crowd of mourners, is slowly borne to an open grave. Cheering words are said as the poor remains are lowered to mingle with the dust of the ages—as one more mortal joins "the innumerable caravan" of the past. But with the trustful eye of hope I behold our friend still standing by our side, drying the tears of the afflicted ones, and stilling the anguish of their suffering souls. The same look of longing, earnest thought which marked the *boy* in the far distant past irradiates the face of the *man*, and the energy by which it was then characterized tells, in tones which cannot be mistaken, that the life which was begun with so much promise and devotion HERE will be rounded and completed THERE !

And so the vision faded from my view ! But as it passed I saw that the tear-drops which had fallen had congealed to pearls of affection, and the flowers had shaped themselves into garlands of memory— in the midst of which I read, in letters of shining gold, the name of

EDWIN ADAMS !

JAMES HAMILTON,

ARTIST.

March 17, 1878.

Far from his home, far from those who were nearest and dearest to him on earth, James Hamilton has passed away! The sudden manner of his taking off has brought with it a shock to those who knew and loved him, and it is hard even now to believe that he, whom, only a week ago to-day, I saw and conversed with, apparently in his usual health, should have journeyed into that mysterious land whose portals are opened only by the finger of Death! The men who, by the power of their genius, dignify and elevate their race, and who become in the best sense its teachers, belong specially to no country, but by the magic power of their minds take all humanity into their embrace, and join all nations in one universal brotherhood! Such men, therefore, are benefactors unknown to themselves; they scatter blessings unwittingly along their pathway, and are entitled to the gratitude of the ages! The death of a great artist is a loss to the world, and the man whose remains lie cold and still before us, was no common man. His genius has made its impress upon the art-history of his

adopted country, and when we, who now assemble
to pay a last tribute of respect to his memory, shall
have passed from earth, the name of James Hamilton will live enshrined in the radiance of an almost
imperishable fame, and his works be treasured
among the greatest triumphs of the painter's skill.
His "Capture of the Serapis," and "Burning of Le
Bon Homme Richard," are historical records of which
America may be justly proud, and upon these alone
the fame of our departed friend may well be permitted to repose. Little is known, even by his most
intimate friends, of Hamilton's early life ; but though
Great Britain claims the honor of his birth, it was in
America that his talent as an artist was fostered and
found that appreciation which is so dear to persist-
ent and struggling labor. For over thirty years of
his life he resided in Philadelphia, and, as you know,
nearly three years since he wandered to these Western shores, on which his career has come to this so
sudden and unlooked-for end. It will be fresh in
your remembrance that when his "Chase of the
Smuggler" was first exhibited in San Francisco, the
lovers of art discovered that a great power had come
among us, and that by his advent the community
had been enriched by the accession of a master-
mind. In this city some of his finest works have
found their proper position, and San Francisco may
well be proud of the homage it has rendered to a
genius so striking and so powerful as his. Had he
been spared, it is probable, from the indications of his

later work, that even grander results than we have yet known would have been given to the world, but they are not needed to insure his fame. Nor was his ability confined to his profession. He possessed a vast fund of varied information, and in his brighter moments was a companion whose brilliancy of conversation won all hearts to him, and can never be forgotten by those who were admitted to an intimacy with him. He numbered among his friends most of the celebrated men and women of his time ; and the late Charles Dickens, Dr. Kane, the Arctic explorer, and Charlotte Cushman always regarded him with the warmest feelings of affection. But he is gone. The skilful hand is cold in death, and the eyes which delighted in the changing aspects of nature will behold them for us no more !

It would be well if we could take leave of him as an artist alone, without a thought of the imperfections of the man. But who of us shall judge him? Beneath the surface of his nature there welled up a spring of tenderness and love for all with whom he came in contact ; and his kind and generous friend, " Grace Greenwood," who, while she knew and prized his genius, knew also the weakness which was his besetting sin, spoke of him to me as a child who needed a stronger will than his own to guide him aright and place him above the temptation he found so hard to withstand. The one stumbling-block of his life has destroyed many a son of genius, but it may be, that in the existence to which he has gone he will see more clearly the imperfections of his career, and be enabled to help some poor, suffering brother contending with the enemy which vanquished *him*.

So let him rest. If we can " point a moral" from the failings of his life, it is well for us to do so, but let us draw the kindly veil of charity over his foibles, and remember only the better nature which was so large a portion of the man before us. While we twine the garlands of memory above his grave, let the sweetness of the flowers bear with them the knowledge only of their beauty and freshness, and teach us to think but of those qualities in the character of our friend which, like them, were lessons of loveliness and goodness, foreshadowing a purity above the grossness of earth,—the links which unite us to the Divine !

JOSEPH MAGUIRE.

March 25, 1878.

There are occasions in which silence is more eloquent than words, in which the memories of the past crowd so closely upon our thoughts that we can hardly realize the passage of the present, and find ourselves shrouded, as it were, in an atmosphere of all-enfolding sorrow. As we stand in that silent, unspeakable grief, beside the cold remains of those we love, and know that the final earthly leave-taking has come for us and them, we seek to blot from our minds whatever harsh or ungentle memories might chance to linger there, like shadows on the sunlight of our life, and to gather up only the tender treasures left to us by the affection of the departed. In the solemn event which has now called us together, we have none of these ungentle memories to put away, no harsh recollections to stifle, as we bid farewell to the loved one lying there. Those who knew him need no feeble words of mine to tell how free he was from every act and thought which could tend to weaken the warm attachment which he inspired among his associates,—an attachment which can find no expression in language; so strong and single-hearted was it, that it made us thank God for life, for it proved to us that there was much that was good in man. No, the sorrowing hearts that now gather with tearful eyes and breasts throbbing with the divinest sympathy of affection around the bier of "poor Joe," can need no recital of his worth, no reminder of his kindly, gentle soul. To them he can never die, for the sweet influence of his life will be to them always an abiding reality, a resting-place for their heart's constant and unchanging love.

> That love will last as pure and whole
> As when he loved us here in time,
> And at the spiritual prime,
> Rewaken with the dawning soul.

But those to whom he was comparatively a stranger, who knew him only at a distance, and who were not permitted a glimpse into the real nature of the man, can hardly realize how noble, how true he was, how utterly free from the petty weaknesses which go to make up a large portion of the character of most of us, and how large and universal was his sympathy with every suffering with which he came in contact. Through long years of the closest intimacy, those who were nearest to him can recall no single unkind thought, no harsh word against another, no uncharitable act to dim the brightness of his generous and unselfish life. Far from rich in the possession of the world's goods, he gave liberally of what he earned to those who needed it, and away in his far-off birthplace beyond the sea, an aged mother, who now sits in the tribulation of

mourning for her beloved and affectionate son,
whose care she was, and in whose behalf the
struggles of his life were made, will miss the generous hand which ministered to her wants, and com-
forted the fading hours of her pilgrimage. But it
may be her happiness and consolation to know that
she has had the honor of giving to the world one of
God's own noblemen, an honest, truthful, and large-
hearted man. And let us hope, that the sorrowing
affection which bursts from the hearts of this assembly may be wafted across the waters to her lonely
dwelling, and, in some sense, serve to still the
anguish of her suffering soul.

It is little more than a week ago that many of us
who meet here to-day were gathered around the
coffin of a son of genius, who had been summoned
somewhat suddenly to his "long home."[1] As is
usual on such occasions, some fitting words were
said, some sweet music sung, and the voice of our
friend was heard in those gentle strains. How little
did we, who listened to its tones of beauty, dream
that it would be for the last time! But alas! it was
so decreed. On the evening of that day he went to
his bed, from which he never rose. Happily, he
suffered but little, if at all, and his death was as we
would have such a death to be. But a short time
before the close, he burst into a strain of melody
such as thrilled the souls of those who heard it,

---

[1] James Hamilton, the artist, at whose funeral services Mr. Maguire
sang one of the hymns. This was the last occasion on which his
friends were privileged to meet him in life.

and can never be forgotten by them. As the spirit parted from its frail tenement the voice grew weaker and weaker, until it faded into silence, and the harmonies of earth were caught up and reëchoed by the angel band which waited on the other side. And so our friend and brother passed away. Pure and noble in his life, beautiful and holy in his death, he journeyed over the mysterious river, borne in the arms of sweet and sacred song. His parting from us realizes to the full the touching lines of an old poet :

> " ' What is that, mother ? ' ' The swan, my love ;
> He is floating down to his native grove ;
> Death darkens his eyes, and unplumes his wings,
> Yet the sweetest song is the last he sings.
> Live so, my son, that when death shall come,
> Swan-like and sweet, it may waft thee home.' "

We are here to-day to pay the last tribute to one we loved so well. The sadness of our hearts is the deepest and most striking evidence of the affection we bore him, and the clasping hand, scarce accompanied by a sound, with which we greet each other, tells more eloquently than speech how bitter is our sorrow ! We take our leave of him on earth, with eyes so dim that we can scarce behold the outlines of that once familiar face, and the " God bless him !" which rises to our tongue, can find no utterance for the sobs which choke our words. But he needs no blessing from us. The Father hath already blessed him in the bestowal of so sweet and sunny a nature as his, and in the wealth of love which he inspired. It is we who are left who need that comfort, and when we say "God bless us and help us to bear the sorrow which has come across our way," let us remember that, though parting is the lot of life, in the rest which must come to all there will be

No more desperate endeavor,
No more desolating "never,"
No more separation—ever—
Over there!

MID–SUMMER "HIGH JINKS,"

INVITATION.

" If thou art worn, and hard beset
   With sorrows that thou wouldst forget ;
   If thou wouldst read a lesson that will keep
   Thy heart from fainting, and thy soul from sleep,
   Go to the woods and hills ! "

BOHEMIAN CLUB ROOMS,
June 6, 1878.

FRIEND AND BROTHER :

The crust in which the selfish struggle of our life too often enwraps
our better nature, and which, year by year, gathers more and more
closely around us, concealing by its gross shadow the light that is
within, needs sometimes a kindly touch for its removal ; and where
can we seek for such tender ministration, as at the hand of our
mother, Nature ?

The glorious old woods invite us with their freshness to shake off
our sorrow with the city's dust, and to enter their grand and solemn
cathedral, where the song of the birds and the ripple of the waters
shall make such music as will inspire and give hope to the sinking
soul ! Come, then, and make merry ; come, with every fibre strung
to its highest pitch, and with your heart prepared for enjoyment ;
come, and for a time scatter to the winds the cares of life, and bury
in the waters of oblivion every sorrow !

Come, for the sake of him who pens these lines, who will soon be
divided from you by the width of the continent, and who longs to
carry with him from the land of his love a crowning recollection of
the many happy hours passed among " good friends and true."

HENRY EDWARDS,
Sire.

ADDRESS.

After many weeks of pleasant suspense, the hour we have looked forward to has arrived, and we meet to-night to hold high festival among the towering giants of these glorious woods. And where can a more fitting hall be chosen, in which to pledge each other in good fellowship, and to extend the kindly greetings which help humanity upon its way? Around and about us are the witnesses of the greatest boon that Heaven can give to man, the constant, faithful evidences of that all-pervading beauty which exists only in the rolling hills, with their ever-changing verdure; the pure, the perfect trees; and beneath them their attendant spirits, the sweet and lovely flowers. Amidst the groves, in which the altars of "God's first temples" sent up their incense to the awaiting throne; away from the clangor of tongues, the restless rush of greed, and the ever-repelling influence of the city's throng, we come to cast off the material elements of our being, to lift ourselves a little higher in the plane of existence, and to taste for a brief period of those delights which well up from the fountain of happiness, whose springs the country alone can supply. Here, in the depth of an almost primeval forest, we feel at once the littleness and the grandeur of our lives. By contrast with the whirl of streets, and the crushing excitement by which most of us are impelled, we are led, by the " peace and holy rest " which here prevail, to pause and ask a question of the better thought within : " Why do we miss the bounties which are so lavishly displayed around us, and which may be had but for the asking? Why do we choose the rougher and more dangerous path, when one of safety and of beauty lies ever before our eyes?" The question can receive but one reply. It is, that the love of wealth has overgrown every true instinct of our being, and that the search for riches is the only one in which the eager, restless spirit of this so-called progressive age finds its fitting exercise. And yet, could all men be animated by the same love of relaxation and enjoyment of Nature's beauties, the world would move as steadily as before, and the needs of life be equally well supplied. Can one of us for a moment doubt that he is better for a closer contact like this with all that is fresh and fair upon the earth's surface,—with the waving woods, the almost holy flowers ; with the trickling dew-drop, and the rustling wind ; with the clearer starlight, and the more cloudless radiance of the sun ? No, there is no man here, who after this slight embrace from the arms of his divine mother, will not return to his daily routine with a fresher heart and brain, and with a tenderer and sweeter feeling for his fellows. I sometimes reverence those men of old who, away from the ever-restless crowd of cities, wandered in silent solitude to the mountain's side or the forest's depth, and shut themselves up to commune with their own hearts and the irrepressible beauty which was so liberally spread before them. Such a life may

be in some sense narrow and contracted; it may
not touch the highest aims of which our being is
capable, but it is surely as pure, as noble, and as
useful, as the constant battle for wealth, fought
upon the ignoble fields of selfishness and wrong.
The trouble of this age is that it is too feverish—
too much given to the whirl and worry of life, and
too little inclined to rejoice in the blessings of a
holiday time!

> " Work, work, work,
> Till the brain begins to swim."

seems to be the motto of the race to-day, and the
wearied spirit finds not the repose it needs until the
hour comes which casts over it the benison of an
eternal rest. What abject folly! What utter want
of sense! The cry of Nature echoes everywhere
through her numberless retreats: " Come, ye
hungry ones; come and partake of the feast I
spread before you. Come, ye who are athirst, and
drink of the fountain of perpetual peace!" And
the wayfarers turn a deaf ear, and pass along to
their early graves, wrapt in the mantle of selfishness
and greed of gain, allowing no ray of beauty from
the light above to penetrate the darkness of their
souls. Will it be for ever thus, and will men always
lose their way in the journey over the clearly
marked pathway of life? I think not so. As year
by year rolls on, it seems to me as if content will be
more readily found; as if the struggles for existence
will be less and less protracted; as if the necessities

of life will be more readily within the reach of all, and the glamour of gold be less and less attractive to men's eyes! A millenium like this is no poet's dream ; it needs but the earnest thought and work of earnest minds in every civilized land, and that perseverance which, while it urges forward a good deed, stimulates by its influence and its example. The want of rest and healthy, hopeful, cheerful enjoyment is the great want of the world to-day, and perhaps in this country, more than in any other, is this want apparent. It is the evil which is destroying the lives of the people,—the cruel cancer which is eating at their very vitals, wasting their energies, and poisoning the life-blood of the race! The teacher who will boldly proclaim this truth, and set before those who come within the scope of his influence the foul and demoralizing effect of this hideous wrong, will earn for himself not only a deathless fame, but the enduring gratitude of the ages.

In more than one sense it is " good for us to be here." If we cannot claim for these solitudes the fame of classic ground ; if we cannot people these leafy glades with a Rosalind and a Touchstone; if we can see not in our fancy the band which followed the bold outlaw, Robin Hood, or hear Fitz-James's bugle call, we yet can mark around us upon every side the changes which have been wrought by the mighty convulsions of the past, and in the spirit of the glorious master, learn by contemplation to

" Find tongues in trees, books in the running brooks,
Sermons in stones, and good in every thing."

To myself, this occasion is fraught with the deepest interest, for I feel that it is the last on which I may meet with many of you, at least under circumstances like the present, and it seems to be one of those special passages in life which mark a sudden and abiding change, as the milestones which proclaim the distances in life's journey appear to us the more rapidly as we approach its close. Nearly six years of delightful association are fast drawing to an end, and the curtain is about to descend upon the pleasant pictures of the past. I am thankful in my own heart that my last remembrance of our many happy gatherings will be connected with this lovely spot, and with the beauty which is everywhere around us. This experience is indeed a source to me of the deepest gratification, and away in a distant home, in the years that are to come, this scene will often recur to my memory, enshrined in the all-enfolding charm which belongs to the vanished hours. I must, however, own, that in the midst of the merriment which I trust is in your hearts there is a tone of sweet sadness in mine, for the severance of ties which have bound me so closely to you all cannot but bring with it a sensation of sorrow, and the wrench which tears me from the association which I have so long been privileged to enjoy, bears its own sense of pain. I cannot but remember, also, that since we first met together and founded the institution which has in so short a time become one of the influential societies of our young State, many of our comrades have gone down in the battle of life, leaving their places unoccupied, and only the recollection of their loving hearts to comfort and console. As those who have laid down their burdens and gone "to their long home" pass in shadowy review before me—you see with me the ranks as they wander by, and hear the murmur of their unspoken voices—"blessings and peace to all." There is no need to breathe their names—they will dwell in your minds for aye, for they were linked to you by bonds which even the bolt of the destroyer had not power to shatter. Nor do I deem it idle to believe that they linger near us to-night full of the enjoyment which this assemblage brings—laughing when we laugh, saddening when we are sad. Oh, no! for as we cast ourselves, as we do to-night, away from the grinding cares of life, and with the tender love of children approach the bosom of our universal mother, we bring nearer and ever nearer to us the life which is beyond, and moving within the sphere of a higher influence, summon about us the love, the watchfulness, and the deathless affection which have "gone before."

"TRIFLES LIGHT AS AIR."

"A snapper-up of unconsidered trifles."

A Winter's Tale.

129

TWO BALLOON VOYAGES.

In the year 1858, the well-known Australian manager, Mr. George Coppin, among the many other attractions which he introduced for the amusement of the good people of "the colonies," imported two large balloons, with their attendants, Messrs. Dean and Brown, two experienced aeronauts, and after some rather unsuccessful attempts in Melbourne, sent them on to try their fortune in Sydney, in which city I was then residing. A considerable sum of money had been expended upon the speculation, and at one time it appeared as if a very heavy loss would be entailed. So that being well known in the New South Wales capital, and prompted by the belief that the confidence which had been somewhat impaired by the comparative failure of the enterprise, might be restored if a satisfactory ascent could be made, the incidents of which could be vouched for by some one outside those more immediately concerned, I volunteered to accompany the aeronauts upon their first voyage. Accordingly, on the 19th of December, the process of inflation took place in the lovely domain of Sydney, and the arrangements for our trip were completed. An immense concourse of spectators was present, but the provisions for keeping the crowd from the immediate vicinity of the balloon were far from complete, and during the swaying of the huge globe, (the result of a high wind blowing at the time,) a large rent was caused in the silk by a looker-on holding up his umbrella to shield himself, as the vast mass turned toward the spot on which he was standing. This allowed the gas to escape, and it was, for a time, feared that the ascent would have to be abandoned, but the rent was soon partially repaired, and more gas being pressed into the balloon, the aeronaut, Mr. Brown, entered the car, I followed ; we were set free, and shot up suddenly to a height of about two hundred feet. But the motive power was insufficient to carry us out of the lower stratum of air, and although the ballast was thrown out almost to the emptying of the car, we could not rise, but were carried rapidly by the wind in the direction of the city. In our course we struck against the pinnacle of a church near at hand, and for a few seconds, (for all this occurred in the space of less than a minute), it seemed as if our time had come. Brown called out to me, "Throw every thing overboard." I obeyed his instructions by pitching out first our lunch-basket and its contents, and then (from what impulse I know not) my coat, overcoat, waistcoat, and hat. A large crowd had followed our course, talking and shouting most vociferously, and increasing the excitement by their half-frantic gestures and tumultuous cries. Among this wild human mass my garments fell, and it should be recorded to the credit of the populace of Sydney that they were all honestly cared for, and with my gold watch which was in the pocket of my vest, restored to me "safe and sound." The balloon being entirely out of control, was dashed hither and thither, striking against chimney tops and other projections, rendering it very difficult for us, even by clinging to the rope, to maintain our position in the car, until in crossing Macquarie Street, a little above the elevation of the tallest houses, the grapnel, which had been thrown out in the chance of fastening somewhere, caught in a window-sill, the ropes we sent over the sides were seized by willing hands, and we descended in safety. We had been, as we afterward learned, only seven minutes in the air, but those seven minutes seemed like a lifetime, and on stepping once more upon *terra firma*, I realized the possibility of the hair turning suddenly white as the effect of an extreme mental strain. Warm hearts and kindly words, however, speedily dispelled our terror, and we were soon once more amongst our friends.

So ended my first balloon voyage; and looking back upon the incident over a lapse of years, I appreciate our wonderful escape, and am thankful that the adventure, though it could but be regarded as a failure of the end in view, had not a termination more painfully terrible. The object of the voyage, however, was yet unaccomplished, and another ascent was quietly proposed, of which no notice was to be given. With something of the foolhardiness which belongs to the early days of life, I determined again to try to "win my spurs," and in opposition to the wishes of my friends, "resolved to do or die." On the 30th of the month the balloon was conveyed to a secluded part of the Government Gardens, and there, by the permission of Sir Wm. Denison, then Governor of New South Wales, it was once more prepared for its lofty flight. The day was such as is only to be found in this lovely climate, clear, bright, and balmy, and at about a quarter-past twelve, accompanied on this occasion by Mr. Dean, I entered the car, the cords which held us to the earth were loosened, and amid the shouts of the excited bystanders, we rose slowly and steadily into the blue, until we attained the height of about half a mile. Here our speed was greatly and suddenly increased by coming in contact with the upper portion of the current of air by which we were carried on our course. In a few minutes we found ourselves immediately over the prison at Cockatoo Island, about two miles in a straight line from the place of our start, and here all motion seemed to cease, and for upwards of a quarter of an hour we were almost stationary. After hearing from my companion that we were all right, and exchanging with him a hearty shake of the hand, I leaned over the side of the car, and gazed, not without a feeling of awe and wonder, upon the scene around and beneath me. Pen and tongue utterly fail to do justice to the sublime spectacle. Long as I had been impressed with the beauty of Sydney, and more especially of the harbor of Port Jackson, I found that until then I knew nothing of the magnificence of this queen of the Southern Hemisphere. The city itself, with its many little points running out into the bay, each one dotted with buildings, looked like a miniature Sebastopol, and though its streets for us no longer bore the signs of their usual stir and bustle; though the forms of those whose eager eyes had watched us from beneath had faded from our view, and the cabs and other vehicles which give so much animation to a city, wore · the aspect of flies of different orders and genera, the hum of thousand voices and thousand sounds fell softly upon the ear, and told us that we were yet within the region of our fellow-men. Rising, however, more and more rapidly, until we attained our greatest altitude, that of about two miles, those sounds gradually ceased, and the most death-like and solemn silence prevailed. So profound indeed was it, and so rarefied the condition of the atmosphere, that the pulsation of my own heart could be distinctly heard; the opening and shutting of the valve sounded like a pistol-shot; and the flirting of the balloon like the flapping of a ship's sail in a gale of wind.

> " Far, far below the chariot's path,
> Calm as a slumbering babe,
> Tremendous Ocean lay,

while immediately beneath our track were spread, like a net-work, the countless creeks, inlets, and bays of the beautiful harbor, and far off in the northern distance we could discern the waters of the Hawkesbury, in their junction with Broken Bay. To the eastward the North and South heads appeared like small projecting fragments of rock, and the " waste of waters " beyond seem to mingle with and lose itself in the clouds. Shark, Clark, and Garden islands were but little patches smaller than one's hand, and the many sandy beaches of the bay like strips of the whitest calico. The vessels at anchor were many of them soon lost to view, and when I last saw her, the " European " steamship looked no larger than the plaything of a child. The almost interminable forests of gum-trees trending toward the north of Middle Harbor, the stretch of orchards of oranges and vines with which the country toward Paramatta is studded, dotted here and there with pretty cottages, rising up among them like daisies upon a green sward, the magnificent reach of undulating land to the base of the Blue Mountains, the grand sight of the cliffs toward Botany, and of that bay itself,—all this must be left to the imagination of those less fortunate than myself, as any attempt at description must utterly fail.

We experienced several trifling changes of current, and at one time our course was directed toward Broken Bay—a fact which excited in my mind my only uncomfortable feeling, as nothing seemed to await us, but the chance of a descent in an almost uninhabited district, and a prospect of lodging beneath the trunk of an ancestral gum-tree. I was all the more anxious, as it was a part of my duty to support Mr. G. V. Brooke in " Love's Sacrifice " the same evening at the Prince of Wales Theatre, and an early return to Sydney was among my calculations when I started upon the trip. After reaching the greatest elevation (before alluded to as that of about two miles), we had gradually descended until the various objects on earth could be clearly distinguished, and in the direction in which we were carried by the wind, we could discern some open patches of land in the neighborhood of Paramatta, in one of which we hoped to make our landing. The grapnel was thrown over, the ropes loosened, the valve opened to allow the escape of the gas, and in a few minutes we descended in an orchard at Kissing Point, near the banks of the Paramatta River. The car struck the ground with considerable force, rebounded, struck again, and the second time the grapnel caught in the branches of an apple tree, and with a few trifling bruises, and some damage to our clothes, we were enabled to alight. The huge machine was emptied of its contents, folded, and placed in the car, and by the kindness of the many people who had assembled to our assistance, it was conveyed to the river's bank, and placed on board one of the steamers plying between Sydney and Paramatta. We reached the city about seven

o'clock, and before eight, I was dressed for " Eugene de Lorme," and was recounting to a generous and partial audience in the greenroom, my adventures of the day. We had travelled about nine and a half miles in a base line, nearly twenty-two, allowing for the variations in our course, and were in the air a little over fifty minutes. There is no sensation of a disagreeable nature in ascending in a balloon, as the occupant of the car appears to be perfectly station- ary, and the earth and all upon it seem to be sink- ing away from him. The temperature was purer and more exhilarating than any I ever before en- joyed ; all sense of fear was lost in the contempla- tion of the majesty around me ; and beyond a pain in the ears, which seized me at our greatest altitude, and which lasted but for a few minutes, I did not experience the slightest feeling of annoyance.

THE CHURCH AND THE STAGE.

A LETTER ADDRESSED TO THE REV'D JOS. BEASLEY, OF
SYDNEY, N. S. WALES, IN REPLY TO A SERMON
ATTACKING THE DRAMATIC PROFESSION,
DELIVERED JULY 25, 1859.

REVEREND SIR:—You last night delivered a lecture at Temperance Hall, on the subject of " Popular Amusements," in the course of which you took occasion to declaim against theatrical representations, as being dangerous to public morals and inimical to the best interests of society. Of course you are entitled to your own individual opinion upon such a matter as this; and however narrow-minded I, as an actor, may think that opinion, I should not thus publicly have ventured to address you, had you been a little more cautious in other of your remarks upon that profession to which I have the honor to belong. But, sir, you have not only uttered bigoted views with regard to what has always, even in the more remote ages of the world, been the most popular means of conveying amusement, blended with instruction of a lofty and refined character; but by saying that " the performers of stage plays were frequently of doubtful virtue," you have cast a slur upon the character of a body of persons whose reputations are as valuable as your own, and offered a gratuitous insult to a large and influential class, who, from the very nature of their profession (engrossing as it does so much time and attention), are never anxious to be drawn into prominence in other ways than in the exercise of their legitimate calling.

There has been of late existing in this city a strong feeling on the part of ministers of various religious denominations against the theatrical profession, and I have been told that these self-styled Christians have frequently denounced from their pulpits, the stage, its followers and its supporters. These displays of priestly eloquence and priestly charity, have been passed over, partly from a desire on the part of the dramatic profession generally to abstain from discusssion on a subject so nearly affecting themselves, and partly from the fact that it has been difficult to found any controversy upon words uttered "viva voce," as they may by chance be wrongly quoted, or subjected to a false interpretation.

But, sir, your address of last night is now public property, and I claim the right to express my views upon the sentiments it contains. Your objections to the theatres are : "The number of public houses and houses of ill-fame which spring up in the neighborhood of theatres ; of the performers being frequently of doubtful virtue ; of the lighter portion of the community, those who felt the importance of divine things the least, being the principal supporters of the theatre.'' On the strength of these assertions, you arrive at the conclusion that theatrical representations are wrong, and hurtful in their tendency. I shall ask your patience while I consider these objections in the light in which they appear to me.

And first, I must observe that you have no foundation on which to build your statement that houses of ill-fame spring up in the neighborhood of theatres. There are at this moment two theatres open in Sydney, both of them, as regards their external appearance, creditable buildings. They are situated in two of the principal streets of the city, and I challenge you to point out any of the houses of the character to which you allude, in their vicinity. That public-houses spring up near theatres is true, but does not the same thing occur near our police-courts, our markets, our custom-houses, our wharves, and all other places in which large concourses of people are daily gathered? And even admitting such to be the case, what has this to do with theatrical entertainments, except as a secondary consequence? The houses used as taverns are licensed by the Government, and are under the continued surveillance of the police, and the evils of such (if any exist) are not arising out of the establishment of the theatres, but from a proper want of attention on the part of the authorities. Surely, sir, you will

admit that around all institutions which are under
the control of erring humanity, some symptoms of
the imperfections of our nature must arise, and I
think you will scarcely deny that even the free and
elevating teachings of Christianity itself are somewhat
altered from the form and spirit in which they existed in the mind of their Divine Author; and I
boldly contend that the evils which spring up in-
directly from large numbers of persons being brought
together in theatres are no more chargeable to the
dramatic art itself, than are the corrupt doings of
some who " call themselves Christians " to be laid
at the door of the faith enunciated by Him who said:
"Thou hypocrite, first cast out the beam out of thine
own eye, then thou shalt see clearly to cast out the
mote out of thy brother's eye ! "

Your second objection is one of a more personal
character; and I can but say, is strongly at variance
with the statement at the commencement of your
lecture, to the effect that you were about to treat the
subject before you as a man, an Englishman, and
a gentleman.   Let me ask you, " Are you personally
acquainted with any members of my profession ? "   I
I assume you are not, and if you are not, it is, at the
least, unmanly to say any thing against them on mere
hearsay, and if unmanly, it is un-English and ungen-
tlemanly too.   If you *are* known to any of the
followers of " the mimic art," you cannot think
them, if you judge aright, worse than others of their
species, and I shall not be charged by many who

know them best, with exaggeration, when I say,
that as a distinct class there are few so thoroughly
free from the vices which commonly beset society.
I am not aware, sir, whether you are cognizant of
the fact, but to the best of my belief there is no
record in the Statute-Book of any one member of
the theatrical profession ever having been convicted
of a capital offence, and the statistics of crime, both
in the mother-country and here, will incontestably
prove, that large as are their numbers, actors and
actresses are very rarely charged, much less convicted of *any* offence against the laws of their country. Can you say as much for your own class?
No, you cannot. I would wish to avoid as much as
possible all personalities, but you have commenced
them ; and " people who live in glass houses,"—you
know the rest. I venture to assert that for one
member of my profession who has during any given
time, say the last half century, figured in our courts
of justice, there have been at least six or seven of
your own calling. This is a bold statement, sir,
but it can be established by proof.

You may have heard—for I question much if you
can speak of us by your own knowledge,—you " may
have heard," I say, that actors have been, at times,
too much given to habits of inebriety; and that actresses have been known to desert their husbands and
form other connections, or, perhaps, that they have
chosen, from motives best known to themselves, to enter virtually upon the state of married life without re-

garding the forms imposed upon that state by the laws
of our existing society. You may have heard all this,
and it may be true. But have you ever given yourself the trouble to think, that as public men and
women who are constantly before the gaze of thousands, their actions are easily made patent to the
world, and that the faults to be laid to their charge
are not only liable to great exaggeration, but that,
if they were committed by other classes of people,
the knowledge of them would be confined to a few,
and society at large would be quite ignorant of them ?
This is a point of view from which I think you
should regard the question of the " doubtful virtue"
of stage performers. I say again and again—and I
challenge contradiction of the assertion—that actors
and actresses generally are more free from the vices
which beset and degrade humanity than any
other class of the same numbers and importance in
the social scale. I do not wish it to be understood
that I think them free from faults, and that they
have no errors to be laid to their charge ; but I do
say, that from the very nature of their profession,
they are so compelled to cultivate the habit of con-
centrating all their mental force upon one given
subject, so inevitably bound to nurse and foster the
gift of memory, and so much occupied with regard
to their time in the study of their art, that by the
constant exercise of the higher faculties of the
mind which are brought into continuous and
harmonious action by such study, the lower qualities

of their nature are kept in abeyance, and are not suffered to put forth their baneful fruits, which, under evil influences, too frequently appear to contaminate and poison society. " Doubtful virtue," forsooth ! I am half inclined to laugh at a phrase which bears so plainly on its surface the marks of bigotry, intolerance, and ignorance. But the consequence of such statements as those which you have made cannot be so lightly passed over. I know that error must eventually give way before the light of truth, and that sentiments like those which you have enunciated must soon be lost in the great vortex of civilization ; but I feel, and I feel warmly, for hundreds of honest, upright, noble-hearted men—and still more for many gentle, excellent, accomplished women,—who can but experience the pangs which must naturally arise from the outrage offered to their feelings by statements like your own, and placing myself thus prominently forward to do battle for the wrongs which have been so wantonly heaped upon the class to which I belong, I am actuated solely by a love of truth, and a conscientious desire to do justice to those to whom, by the intolerance of many persons of confined and sectarian views, it has been ruthlessly and uncharitably denied. I ask you, sir, as a Christian minister, to reconsider what you have said, and what has gone before the world, and when you are again about to put forth your views with regard to the character and conduct of your fellow-mortals, to pause for a moment and reflect upon the saying of Him, whose faith you profess to teach—whose rules of life you profess to follow,—" Let him that is without sin cast the first stone."

With regard to your third objection, viz.: " That theatres are principally supported by those who feel the importance of divine things the least," I shall say but little.   Perhaps you and I may differ in our views as to what may be the proper manner in which the importance of divine things may be felt ; but it certainly appears to me that the amusement which has for ages secured the approbation of the great and good of every country and people, has not been permitted by the Great Author of divine things himself to exist so long as it has done, and the love for such amusements to be regarded as a natural craving of the human heart, without exerting some beneficial tendency ; and when, not to wander from home, I see the great mass of visitors to theatrical representations in Sydney, composed of the most respectable and influential inhabitants of the city, I humbly confess I am glad to have my views in the matter endorsed by so many respectable persons, and am content to follow in their wake as to the importance of " divine things."

In your lecture you stated that you had never until last week attended an oratorio, much less is it possible you can have been within the precincts of a theatre. Shall I be deemed impertinent if I advise you to go and see for yourself what theatres are like ? I trust I shall not, for I feel that a few visits to a respectable theatre would, if you went with an unbiassed mind, change the tone of your opinions with regard to the amusements presented there. But if you will not go, then be assured that attacks upon the stage and its professors, made by yourself and persons holding opinions in harmony with your own, will avail but little, and in the waste of your mental strength you will make no more progress among the hearts of society with your dogmas, than did Sisyphus of old with the stone up the mountain side.

A few words more and I have done; I have not sought this quarrel with you; I know you not, and toward you individually I have no ill-feeling. It is against your opinions that I have taken my stand; and though I trust I may never again be placed in a position to call forth any remarks of mine on the subject of this letter, be assured I shall not shrink if the time and occasion should arrive, but shall be ever on the watch to do battle for that art of which I am an humble follower, and for those who, like myself, are anxious to see it placed in the position which it ought to hold amongst the instructive and elevating influences which aid and direct the progress of the human mind.

AGASSIZ.

DIED Dec. 14, 1873.

"Oh! what a noble heart was here undone,
  When Science self destroyed her favorite son."

From a seat of learning in the North has gone forth a wail of sorrow, a wail which echoes not only through the length and breadth of our own land, but in every place in which refinement and culture have found a home, and which will thrill for years to come in many a heart at the mention of the name of the departed. Agassiz is dead. The mighty brain in which grand thoughts were kindled is, as far as our earth is concerned, at rest forever; the smile which ever shone on modest merit beams for us no more; the kind and gentle voice which spoke in earnest sympathy with even the meanest endeavor, is hushed and still, and memory is all that is left us of one so loved. To speak in praise of his vast acquirements would be but

"To guard a title that was rich before."

The history of his adopted country will inscribe them on its brightest pages, and his works will be forever cherished amid the records of the nation. But apart from the homage which the worshippers of his genius will surely lay before its shrine,—apart from the consideration of the labors which have rendered him immortal, and enrolled his name among the deathless few,—there steals into the thought the recollection of that tender and gentle nature which was so magnetic in its association, and which shed so pleasing an influence upon all who came within its contact. Involved in his own cherished pursuits, he scorned the mean pretences of the world, and being, as he himself declared, "Too busy to make money," he was utterly free from the taint of selfishness, and lived less for his own advancement than for the good of others, preferring the calm enjoyment of a studious and retiring life to the tinsel glories of wealth and display. Mindful of the difficulties which beset the student of science, and well knowing how willingly the world will sneer at what it cannot comprehend, his hand was ever extended to help the seeker after truth, and to place his feet upon a firm foundation. A father among the young, a brother among the mature, and a kind and gentle friend to all, the name of Agassiz will be loved as his genius is honored, and his childlike nature cherished as his mental powers are valued and esteemed. Above the earth which covers his remains will be mingled the bitter regrets for the loss of one so gifted, and the sighs of sympathy for those who will miss the communion of a loving heart. As on and on we journey toward the end, the pathway of our life is strewn with sorrowing memories; but the blossoms of existence diffuse their fragrance by the wayside, and teach us that all is not sad for those who mourn. The incense of good deeds ascends to Heaven, and the place which so glorious a soul as his filled on earth, becomes a monument for after-time, and points to the generations which follow the shining remembrance of his power. For over fourteen years the writer has held pleasant intercourse with him, has profited by the varied store of knowledge he was ever so ready to impart, and with a saddened soul would add this poor tributary leaf to the garlands which will deck his tomb. He is but one among the many who have felt the friendly interest which Agassiz was wont to display to all who needed the help of such a teacher, and who, in the years to come, will sigh

> " For the touch of a vanished hand,
> And the sound of a voice that is still."

MAJOR HARRY LARKYNS.

The melancholy circumstances surrounding the death of Major Larkyns, which took place in October, 1874, are so fresh in the recollection as to need no further mention here. But the present opportunity is taken advantage of to allude to his great abilities, and to regret that the influences about him were such as to fetter their fullest action, and to prevent him from adorning more distinctly the walk of life in which he moved. Poverty always hung like a gaunt spectre about his footsteps, and the generous fountains of his nature were dried up by her touch. He walked among men as if they knew him not, and it was only the few who were admitted to a close intimacy with him who felt the warmth of that heart which showed its secrets but so rarely. He was an admirable linguist, familiar with the literature of most continental nations,—a brilliant writer, to whom no theme appeared to come amiss,—a musician of culture,—an artist of refined and polished taste,—and, as a conversationalist rarely excelled. Beyond all these, he was a warm and true friend, and where his sympathies were aroused, his generosity led him often far beyond the bounds of prudence. Many a story of his kindness to those in want is well known to his associates, and the recollection of his unselfish character is with them a sacred memory. He was followed to the grave by many who knew and loved him, and whose appreciation of his worth was evident by the depth of their sorrow. At the close of the religious ceremonies, the following remarks were made :

Friends :—I little thought when, less than three weeks ago, I clasped hands with him and bade him God-speed upon the work he had just undertaken, that I should so soon have been called upon to stand beside the dead body of Harry Larkyns and pay this last sad tribute to his memory. And I know that in a moment like the present I may claim and receive the sympathy of those around me, for here are gathered those who loved him well, and to whom my poor words can convey but little meaning. Still it is good to be here. It is good for us to linger for a moment about his remains, and from the grave which soon will cover them to pluck a blade of memory, greener than the grass ; to weave it into a chaplet of sorrow lighter than the air ; to waft it upon the current of our sympathy over land and sea to the home of his birth, and laying it with the tenderness of our pity at the feet of the mourning ones who loved and cherished him, say, in all the grand fraternal feeling of sorrow : " Though you were absent he was not alone, for man's grief and woman's tears attended him to the last, and he sleeps in peace, for gentle and loving hands have laid him in his grave." Of him who now lies cold and still before us what shall we say ?

We who knew him best, knew well the struggle of his life, the torments he endured, the wearying conflict of his one poor heart against a world of selfish, pitiless pride ; a pride so pitiless that a single tone of manly friendship or a word of womanly sympathy came to him like an echo of the voices which he heard in childhood,—voices which he longed again to hear, but which he resolved never more to listen to until the thorny path which misfortune had placed before him had been cleared by the energy of his own endeavor, and he could stand proudly before those loved ones of an earlier time and say : " I bring you back the honor you bestowed upon me, unstained as when it left your hands, and claim, in common justice to my nature, a full oblivion of the past." He was a gentleman in the truest sense of the word. Upon his lips the breath of slander never lived, the cruelty of corrupting tongues never found a home ; vulgarity of every kind was a perfect stranger to his soul, and in the retrospect of his own sorrows he knew how to find excuses for the follies of his fellow-men, and to cover with the mantle of charity those errors which the world too often blackens with the name of crime. A soldier by profession, distinguished upon the battle-field, the grandest and most heroic struggles of his life were the hand-to-hand conflicts which he waged against those who reviled him here and who were far beneath him in every point of manliness and truth and honor. And now that he is dead, let those detractors know, that no mother's tender hand ever smoothed his head, no father's gentle voice ever offered him counsel. Those natural protectors and advisers were snatched from him at so early an age that his memory of them was but a faded recollection. Deprived of their care and protection he had to fight the battle of his life alone. How nobly he struggled, how grandly he toiled, we, who knew his sacrificing heroism can testify, and the number of those who loved and honored him, and who are to-day gathered in the depth of sorrow around his poor remains, will be the best evidence of the affection he inspired, and of the regrets at his unhappy death which are now breathed above his tomb.

And now, gentle and loving friend and brother, farewell! The blessing of eternal rest has fallen upon your soul! Is it too much to hope that in your home of peaceful calm, your spirit now hears the words of the friend who loved you well, and still more the unspoken sorrow of those who stand around your bier, and that their love and regard may testify to you how bitter is their grief at their untimely loss, and how deep the affection with which they will cherish your memory in the years which are yet to come?

WILLIAM BARRY,

COMEDIAN OF THE CALIFORNIA THEATRE, DIED
JANUARY 2, 1875.

Amid the various scenes of which the drama of this our life is composed, sadness and sorrow have oftentimes a place, and the mask of revelry and gladness frequently hides a face which, when stripped of its covering, wears an aspect of the deepest gloom. Gathered close around the body of him whose soul was consecrated to mirth we feel how intimately in our existence the serious and the grotesque, the pathetic and the ludicrous are blended together, and we, who only a few evenings since laughed with delight at the sallies of his wit, are now come to weep above his coffin. The grave which he has so often dug in sport for the reception of a mimic corpse, has now in truth been opened for him, and the cold clods of earth must soon cover his remains. His taking off has been most sudden and warningless, and passing away alone, with no friend near to close his eyes and whisper a word of loving comfort, the shock of his hasty death has fallen with a withering blight upon the hearts of his associates, who only a few evenings since saw him in apparently vigorous health. But even in this somewhat unheralded departure there is consolation. He writhed under no pain, he suffered not from any mental torture, but passed away peacefully, as to a pleasant sleep. The hand of "God's gentle angel," that leads us with a tender touch into that mysterious realm which is the common heritage of us all, and which, even for the best and strongest of us, must in a few brief years be opened to our knowledge, has beckoned him away from earth, and closing behind him " the great gateway of the past," has shut out forever the influence of sorrow and suffering and wrong. Of his talents in that walk of his profession to which he of late years devoted himself, it is hardly needful that I should speak. They were of that remarkable character that they could not fail to leave an impression upon the minds of those who experienced their power, and have established for him a reputation, both lasting and extended. When the history of the California stage shall be written, the name of William Barry must embellish its brightest page, and in the temple consecrated to dramatic art the laurels which adorn his brow must long remain fresh and green. Conscientious and earnest in the work before him, he was pre-eminently a master of his peculiar branch; and while he always endeavored to bring to the study of a character all the adornments it had received from his predecessors, he invariably invested it with a feeling and power exclusively and singularly his own; and it is not too much to say that he bridged over the gulf which separates the present school of acting from the more thoughtful and labored style of the past, and that in him we have lost one of the last links in the chain which bound us to the stage traditions of our fathers. But you who knew him so well and so long, know also his shining merits as an artist, and my words can add but little to the hold they will have upon your memory. If he had a fault it was one which never pressed hard upon another, but was an injury to himself alone, and the gentleness of his heart, his quiet and inoffensive manner, childlike and innocent in its every expression, while it allowed no wrong to others to come within its influence, should teach us to look kindly and with sorrow upon the one weakness of his life. The regret among his comrades, and the sympathy of loving hearts outside of his profession, evidenced by the gathering now present, are the surest proofs of the love he always inspired, and of the respect which all who knew him are now so desirous to display. And though we take leave with sadness of his earthly form, in spirit he will be long and constantly with us, who believe

> " That our remembrance, though unspoken,
>   May reach him where he lives " ;

and in many an hour to come will tender and affectionate tribute be paid to his memory, mingled with a soft and gentle grief that we can know him on earth no more.